Weight of The Badge

The Sisters, Texas Mystery Series

Book 17

BECKI WILLIS

CONTENTS

Weight of The Badge i
  The Sisters, Texas Mystery Series i
  Book 17 i
BECKI WILLIS i
CONTENTS 1
  1 1
  2 10
  3 21
  4 30
  5 38
  6 44
  7 56
  8 65
  9 73
  10 83
  11 91
  12 102
  13 112
  14 122
  15 132
  16 143
  17 154
  18 166
  19 176
  20 185
  21 194
  22 204
  23 214
  24 225
Note from the Author 234
ABOUT THE AUTHOR 236

This book is dedicated to all first responders who put the safety and wellbeing of others before their own needs.

We owe a debt of gratitude to you all!

1

"I-I need your help!" The woman's words came out in a panic.

"That's what we're here for," Madison deCordova said, her smile conveying through the phone line. "This is Madison. What can I do for you?"

"You can keep me from killing someone, that's what!"

A momentary frown crinkled Madison's brow. People often confused *In a Pinch Professional Services* with a private detective agency. Her rate was less than half that of a PI, even though the jobs were often the same. Tailing a 'victim' to prove insurance fraud; doing the legwork for actual detectives, be it private or for the police department; proving a person innocent of the crime they were suspected of; keeping tabs on a spouse suspected of cheating. Perhaps that's where this conversation was heading, as in 'if he's cheating on me, I swear I'll kill him!'

Madison almost chuckled because no one ever meant such a threat. "Before we go any further, I need to point out that I'm not a marriage counselor, nor am I private investigator." She had to throw it out there, just so the woman understood the limitations of her services.

"Fine, because I don't need either one," the woman snapped. "I need someone to stop me before I do something I'm going to regret."

Madison sobered at the sharp edge in her caller's voice. Cautiously, she asked, "Can you be more specific?"

"I told you. I'm going to kill someone."

Madison sat up straighter in her chair. "Ma'am, this sounds more like a matter for my husband. Have you called the police?"

"I can't! They'll think I'm crazy."

"My husband is the chief of police here in The Sisters. I can promise that he'll listen to you. He doesn't make rash judgments."

"No. I can't go to the police," the woman said adamantly. "That's why I called you. I thought maybe *you'd* help me." Her accusation was clear.

Madison scrambled for a second chance. "Tell me more. Maybe I can help you, after all."

She heard the immediate suspicion in her caller's voice. "Only so that you can turn me in!"

"No. I promise to hear you out."

"How do I know I can believe you?"

"You called me, right?" Madison kept her voice non-confrontational. "You must have believed you could trust me, or else you wouldn't have asked for my help."

"I guess." The woman sounded doubtful.

"Let's start with why you think you might harm someone."

"It's—It's a feeling that overcomes me." The woman struggled to find the right words. "Rage. Hatred. I don't understand it. I don't want it. But it's there, and it's getting worse."

Madison nibbled on her lip. She had no doubt the

caller was sincere. She was clearly distraught. For whatever reason, the woman believed she might do harm, or worse, to another human being. It was a cry for help. Madison wasn't a qualified professional able to help her, but she was a mother. She knew the key was to keep the woman talking, to keep her focused on seeking help rather than giving into her impulses.

"Okay, so that's something," Madison said encouragingly. "You don't want to actually hurt this person, but you're angry. That's understandable."

"No, it's not," the woman argued. "I don't even understand why I'm angry. I just know that I am."

This was the trickiest part of all, so Madison proceeded with care. "Can you tell me who it is that you want to hurt?"

"You don't understand. I don't want to hurt them. I want to kill them." She made the chilling statement with deadly calm.

Her cold demeanor left Madison stunned. Swallowing a gasp, she tried again, knowing fully well her voice shook. "Can—Can you tell me who it is you want to kill?"

"That's just it! I have no idea!"

With that very provocative statement, the woman abruptly hung up.

"Wait! Don't go!"

It was too late. The line had already been cut.

That wasn't the worst part.

The worst part was that she hung up before Madison thought to ask the woman's name.

The call haunted her for the rest of the day. She hit redial, but no one picked up. When she punched it into a reverse look-up search app, the name came back *Unlisted.* She thought of calling Brash, but Madison had given her word that she wouldn't go to the police.

Not without hearing what her caller had to say.

Besides, the woman was right. The police, even the very reasonable Brash deCordova, would think the unknown woman was crazy if she went to them with the same preposterous statement she made to Madison.

As strange as it seemed, however, Madison believed her caller. She believed the woman was genuinely frightened of her own thoughts. The woman was terrified of what she might do, and so was Madison. It was crucial she find this woman and help her.

Madison could think of no other way to put it; the woman had sounded *possessed*.

Before she involved the officials, Madison wanted to find the woman who called. She was curious about the women's story. There had to be more, and Madison wanted to hear it.

What could make the woman think like that? She wondered. *Drugs? Mental illness? A psychotic mind?*

"No," she reasoned aloud, "psychopaths have no conscience. They feel no remorse for their deeds. They wouldn't call and ask for help, not when they relish doing what they do."

The knowledge made her feel somewhat better, but that didn't mean trying to help didn't come without risks. Illegal drugs—even an adverse reaction to a prescribed medication—could make a person behave erratically. The same was true of mental illness. Madison could be inviting danger into their lives by taking on this new client.

"You haven't committed to helping yet," she reminded herself. "And you can't, not unless she calls back." She tapped her fingers on the desk, weighing her options before deciding, "If she does, I'll hear her out. If her story sounds plausible and doesn't create an immediate threat, I'll decide at that point on how to proceed."

If and until that time came, there was nothing else she could do. She had no idea who the woman was or how to get in touch with her.

Madison tried putting the incident out of her mind, but it wasn't easy. She knew she had failed when Brash came home and immediately recognized her worried expression.

"Sweetheart?" he asked, appearing at the doorway into her office. Before the stately old mansion's remodel, the paneled walls and built-in bookcases had housed the formal library. It had a fresh new look now, yet somehow maintained the aura of dignity and grace. "You're still working?" The answer was obvious, but he asked anyway.

Madison lifted her head in surprise. "What time is it?"

"Almost six thirty."

"You're kidding! I completely lost track of time."

"So, I see," he said with a faint smile. She had been engrossed in her computer when he came in, and her hair was mussed. The pattern suggested she had run her fingers through her hair more than once or twice. Most telling was the way she nibbled her lower lip. "What has you so worried?"

Her hazel eyes narrowed. "Who said I was worried?"

"Me."

She thought of making excuses but knew he would see through them. Instead, she shut down her computer and answered honestly, "I had an unusual request by a potential client today. I keep thinking about it."

"Anything I can help with?"

"Not really, but thanks for asking."

"You know I'm here to support you, even though I

don't always agree with you and your zany clients."

Having crossed the room, she slid her arms around him and lifted her face for a kiss. "I know that, and I appreciate it." After a lingering kiss, she leaned back in his arms and admitted, "I didn't start anything for dinner."

"No problem. I can stir up something, or we can go out."

"You look as distracted as I am. Rough day?"

"Like a boat tossed around on a stormy sea." His stomach rumbled in hunger. "On second thought, ax the cooking part. *New Beginnings* or *Montelongo's*?" In a small community like The Sisters, those were their only options for a sit-down meal.

"There's meatloaf left over from last night. What about we make sandwiches and stay in?"

They held hands as they made their way to the far side of the house. Married for almost three years and they still acted like newlyweds.

"Sounds perfect. I'm too tired to go back out, anyway," Brash admitted.

"I hoped things would ease up now that you've hired a third deputy."

Combined, the towns of Juliet and Naomi had a census of under three thousand people, but that didn't mean their police department wasn't overworked and understaffed. Madison worried that her husband worked too much.

"Me, too," he said ruefully. "But even with Nate coming on-board, we're barely treading water."

"How's he doing on the job? Are you still pleased with him?"

"Absolutely. He may be fresh out of the academy but he's sharp and he's eager to learn. He has plenty of energy, too. I can't say that about Perry, and I sometimes wonder about Schimanski."

Madison's snort was far from lady-like. "Otis Perry is like a hundred, and his sidekick isn't exactly a spring chicken."

"Perry is younger than Granny Bert, you know."

"Not a glowing endorsement," she pointed out, "since my grandmother is eighty-three."

"Both are a long way from the century mark."

"There's always the blond bombshell." Madison smiled sweetly, batting her eyelashes in exaggeration. "Misty is certainly younger."

"Abraham is almost my age, but don't tell her I told you."

"You just turned forty-five. You're not ancient by any means."

"No, but Nate Stone can still run circles around me," Brash admitted on a chuckle.

"I highly doubt that, but I agree it must be nice to have some fresh energy on the department." She slid a sly eye toward him. "Megan thinks so, too."

Brash groaned, as she had known he would. "Please, don't remind me. I'm not ready for my baby to have a serious crush on someone."

"Your 'baby' is all grown up. And this is hardly her first crush, nor her first boyfriend."

"According to Megan, they're just 'talking'— whatever that means—and not actually dating," he clarified. "But it was easier to ignore her previous crushes than it is to ignore someone I work with on a daily basis."

"Are you sure that's not part of the problem?"

"Meaning?"

"Maybe," she speculated, "you're uneasy because Nate is older than her other boyfriends. He's probably close to twenty-four or five, right?"

"He is." Brash looked none too happy making the admission.

"He's a man, and in your eyes, she's just a baby."

His only reply was a grunt.

"Megan has a good head on her shoulders. Give her credit for being able to make sound decisions."

"I know you're right, but let's not talk about it tonight. Let's just have a quiet night in, relax, and leave all our worries behind us."

As wonderful as it sounded, the relaxed evening didn't lead to a relaxing night.

Around two o'clock in the morning, Brash's phone rang, disrupting their sleep. Madison stirred, knowing that at two in the morning, it was never good news.

After a brief exchange, Brash ended the call and slid into his jeans.

"What's wrong?" she asked, propping herself up by the elbows.

"There's been another attack," he said tersely.

"That's horrible! What happened this time?"

"A firefighter was shot."

Clutching her chest, she gasped. "Not—"

He read her mind. "No, not Cutter."

"Thank God," she said. Relief washed over, knowing their friend was safe. Guilt took over, because the same might not be true for someone else. "Who?"

"A firefighter on the Riverton VFD."

"What is going on, Brash? Why is someone doing this?"

"If I knew that, maybe I could stop this SOB from hurting someone else." Fastening his service belt around his trim waist, he leaned down to kiss her. "Go back to sleep, sweetheart. No telling what time I'll be in."

"Be safe!" she called after him.

With a heavy sigh, she reached for the electronic reading device she kept by her bed. She didn't think going back to sleep was an option. Not with her husband investigating another random attack in their small community.

She dared not think about it, but some part of her unconsciously worried that Brash could be next.

2

After three attacks, Brash thought he saw a pattern forming.

He pondered the fact as he headed out in the middle of the night.

The first victim had been a River County deputy. While checking out reports of a prowler, someone had ambushed him from behind, hit him over the head with a blunt object, and left him for dead. He was recovering in a College Station hospital but had no clear recollection of the event. Even if his memory did return, he probably hadn't seen his attacker and therefore couldn't describe him.

The second victim was a paramedic with The Sisters EMS. Responding to the report of an injured motorist parked along the side of the road, the ambulance sped to the rescue. They found an abandoned vehicle and called off the responding officer, who happened to be Brash. On their way back to the box, someone fired shots at them. The female medic was injured when she took a slug in the calf of one leg.

When Brash ran the plates, he discovered the car was stolen. It was possible that the shooter only meant to scare off the medics while making his escape, but hitting one with a bullet took the case to a new level. Brash was investigating the shooting as a possible homicide attempt, despite the scant facts surrounding the incident. The call couldn't be traced, and there were no eyewitnesses.

And now, a third victim was injured. While responding to a triggered smoke alarm via its emergency backup system, a volunteer firefighter had been shot in the chest. Medics were still on the scene, trying to stabilize him enough to fly.

Until tonight, Brash had no proof the first shooting and the ambush were related, no matter how much his gut instinct protested. Even this third attack wasn't definitive proof of a connection, but he definitely saw a pattern forming.

All three attacks had been erroneous distress calls. Dedicated first responders had rushed to the scene of each, only to come under attack. Three attacks, three injuries. There had to be a connection.

A black male deputy.

A white female emergency technician.

A Hispanic male who volunteered his time as a firefighter.

Different ethnicities, different sexes, different ages, different backgrounds.

The only thing they appeared to have in common was the badge they wore, whether physically or symbolically. Brash's gut told him their status as first responders was the thread tying all three cases together.

"Not on my watch," he swore grimly. He was the only person inside the SUV, but it didn't dilute the venom in his voice. As chief of police in The Sisters and a special investigator for the county, all three crimes felt personal to him. "Not on my watch."

He arrived at a small gas station just off a blacktopped farm road running between The Sisters and Riverton. Technically, the rural area fell within the county sheriff's jurisdiction but as he was the closest to the mom-and-pop business, he was the first on scene.

Brash took charge, but his first concern was for the fallen volunteer.

"What's the situation?" he asked.

A second ambulance had arrived on his bumper. Running across the parking lot, the paramedics didn't wait to hear the answer. As soon as they reached the patient, they fell onto their knees and went to work, assisting the two medics already working on the pasty-faced fireman. All four worked frantically, but even Brash could see it was a losing battle. No one could lose that much blood and survive. It leaked from his wound faster than they could pump it in through a straight-line catheter.

A fellow firefighter answered, her skin almost as pale as her comrade's. "N-Not good. He's lost a lot of blood, and his pulse is weak. His, uh, blood pressure is falling." She put her hand over her mouth, holding in the horror unfolding before her eyes.

"Can you tell me what happened?" Brash asked. "Maybe over there, so we're not in their way?" After leading her a few feet away, he strategically put himself between her and direct sight of her friend.

"The, uh, the smoke alarm's back-up called in detection," she explained. "Jose, George, and I were the first to arrive at the station, so we brought the big engine. We didn't see smoke, but sometimes it's around back, you know? And—And it was dark, so without flames... Anyway, Jose"—she faltered saying his name— "went around the building and-and someone just opened fire! At the second shot, we heard him yell. He came st-stumbling around the building..." She broke off, unable to go on as she clamped both hands over her mouth and sobbed.

Brash placed a gentle hand on her shoulder. "It's okay. I understand how hard this must be. But whatever you can tell me will be vital in finding this person and bringing him to justice. You think you can do that for me?"

The woman nodded. "I-I'll try."

"Good. First of all, what's your name?"

"D-Dana. Dana Woolrich."

"Okay, Dana, so what can you remember? When you first pulled up, did you see any lights? Movement of any kind?"

"I, uh, don't think so. I know we didn't see smoke. We didn't hear the alarm. One of us—I think maybe it was George—said it must have been a false alarm. But we still have to check it out, you know?"

"Of course. What about as you split up? Any sound of movement then? Anything that seemed unusual?"

Dana scrunched her forehead in thought. Unable to see through Brash's broad shoulders, her eyes kept darting her eyes toward the medics. "It-It was two in the morning. I was still half asleep." Running an unsteady hand through tangled curls, she shook her head dejectedly. "I'm sorry. I can't think of anything."

"That's okay, Dana. You're doing great. I know it's hard, but I want you to think about when the first shot rang out. Where were you? Where was George?"

"I, uh, was at the front door. There was a dim light on in the back, but I, uh, didn't see any smoke. No flames. George had gone around one side, Jose the other. They would circle the building and-and meet me back at the door."

"Was the door locked?"

She finally had an opportunity to nod. "Yes. I tried it, but it didn't open."

"Did you hear anything other than the shot? What

about afterward? Did you hear anyone moving, anyone running?"

Dana was clearly in shock. "George, maybe?" She said it like it was a question. "He was coming around that side of the building when-when we heard the second shot. Th-Then Jose... he came-he came staggering around the building, and... there was so much blood! So. Much. Blood."

Behind Brash, one of the paramedics cried out in panic, "We're losing him!"

Brash was vaguely aware of the frantic movements behind him, and the sound of more sirens approaching. He had his hands full when Dana registered their words and crumpled. As he scooped her up and saved her from hitting the ground, a third firefighter ran up to help. Together, they led the distraught woman to the firetruck where two other firefighters were hunched around it.

All were in shock as the medics hung their heads in defeat and covered their patient's body with a cloth.

With more officers arriving, Brash knew he had to preserve the scene and any evidence there might be. It was likely the EMTs and responding firefighters had already trampled some of it, but he would do what he could to save the rest.

A county deputy arrived and gladly deferred to Brash for instructions. When Otis Perry appeared moments later, Brash ordered both men to establish a boundary around the property. Even when the business owners arrived in their pajamas, they weren't allowed through the perimeter.

By the time the sheriff arrived, Brash had taken crime scene photos and interviewed George Cantrell and the first paramedics on scene.

"Excellent job, deCordova," Sheriff Larson said. "I'll take over the scene, and you can continue collecting evidence and investigating what happened here. I want this person brought in."

"No more than I do, Sheriff. We're a small county. In less than a month, a deputy, a medic, and a firefighter have all been targets. I think these seemingly random attacks are connected. I believe first responders are being targeted as a whole, no matter which badge we serve."

The sheriff considered the theory for only a moment. "I think you could be right. Let's have a meeting in my office. Say noon? We'll order lunch in and take a deeper look into all of this."

"Sounds like a plan."

"There's no moon out tonight. You couldn't see a bleeding elephant as dark as it is. We'll keep the scene secure if you want to head on home and get some rest."

Brash looked toward the sheet-shrouded body being lifted onto a gurney. "I may do that, sir, but not until they remove the body. It's no less respect than he deserves."

A half hour's drive from The Sisters, Riverton was the county seat and home to the jail, the courthouse, and all county offices, including the sheriff. It was also the largest town in River County but considering that all of the towns were small—some downright tiny, in fact—that wasn't saying much. They did have more businesses, however, including more choices on where to eat.

As promised, Sheriff Larson ordered lunch from one of those choices and had it delivered for his noon meeting with Brash.

Brash eyed the elaborate spread with skepticism. "That fresh night air must have had a major effect on your appetite, DeWalt."

Larson chuckled. "I hope you don't object, but I've invited a couple of other chiefs from area towns to join us. The sooner we come up with a plan to find this person, the better. I believe there's one of them, now. Oh, and the other, as well."

As two men walked through the door, Larson greeted them with a handshake. "Gentleman, I believe we all know one another. Let's fix a plate and gather around the table before we start this discussion."

The men exchanged handshakes and general pleasantries as they filled their plates with standard barbecue fare: sausage, beef, or chicken with all the trimmings, accompanied by potato salad and baked beans. A peach cobbler waited to top off their meal.

Once they began eating, the sheriff handed the meeting over to Brash. "Chief deCordova has a very interesting theory concerning the recent violent crimes committed across the county. Brash, I'll let you explain if you don't object."

"Not at all." He tucked his napkin beneath his plate, motioning for the others to continue eating. "As we all know, there's been three random attacks in as many weeks. Deputy Clemens, EMT Sloan, and now, volunteer fireman Jose Robles. I believe the three crimes are connected."

"I don't see how," Riverton Chief of Police Manning replied. "They have nothing in common. Clemens is a middle-aged black deputy. Sloan is a mature white female medic. From what I understand, Robles, a Hispanic fireman, was in his twenties. Those are completely different profiles."

It wasn't the first time Brash and the Riverton PD hadn't seen eye to eye. As a special investigator for the county, Brash was often asked to consult on cases that overlapped within their jurisdiction. They seemed to take it as a personal affront to their own capabilities. A recent case involving one of Madison's clients was proof of their poorly veiled animosity, when Manning's detectives had looked at her as a suspect.

"Hear him out, Bob. He has a good point," the sheriff insisted. "We live in a county that has more square acreage than it does citizens. Even if these crimes didn't include all of our jurisdictions, which they do, we would still need to work together for the greater good of River County. I wanted us all here so that we could look at it from all angles, all viewpoints, and all available resources." He turned back to Brash. "You were saying?"

"From a personal standpoint, you're right, Bob. They don't appear to fall into the same sociological circles. But they do have one thing in common," Brash said.

The fourth man was the chief of police in Cougar Springs. He agreed with Brash and said so. "I think you're right. They're all public servants. They all wear a badge of some sort."

"That's right, Waylon. I think that's the common denominator. I think it's not aimed so much on the victims personally, as it is on their occupation."

"I don't know," Bob argued stubbornly. "Say that to the Robles family and see what kind of reaction you get. I imagine our victims and their families take it pretty personal."

"I would imagine they do. Many victims feel they're in some way responsible for the crimes committed against them, when often nothing could be further from the truth. And I understand that. But we have to approach this from an analytical standpoint, not an emotional one." Brash looked the man across from him straight in the eye. Bob Manning was the only one among them wearing a typical black uniform. There was nothing wrong with dressing like the officer he was, but for him it was a status symbol. It was more a demand for attention than it was homage to his profession. "And while I would certainly word it differently to the Robles family, I think they would find comfort in knowing Jose wasn't murdered by an enemy. Jose did nothing to provoke this killer, other than to serve his community."

Bob clung to his stance. "We don't even know if there *is* a killer." Seeing the argument on all his companions' lips, he corrected himself. "An intentional killer, that is. It could very well be that he only meant to scare the firefighters off, and his shot went astray. It could have been an unintended consequence."

"That's the point, Bob. Actions have consequences." Brash pushed his plate away, having lost his appetite at the other lawman's cavalier attitude. "I don't know about you gentlemen, but I, for one, am investigating the incident in The Sisters as a possible homicide attempt. When I find the perpetrator—and I will— I'll push for the DA to prosecute it as such. Firearms 101: Never aim a gun unless you're prepared to shoot. And never discharge a firearm unless you're prepared to kill."

Tension charged the air after Brash's statement. Sheriff Larson allowed it to hang there, obviously hoping it was long enough to sink into Bob Manning's thick skull. After a significant silence, he picked up the meeting.

"I invited you all here because I agree with Chief deCordova. I think we should look at these crimes as a possible attack on the badges we all wear. It's no secret that there's been a lot of negative publicity toward officers of the law. Some of that is well deserved, but the truth is that the corrupt officers are by far the minority. The overwhelming majority of lawmen are good, decent people dedicated to the public they serve.

They put the welfare of the people before their own preservation. That, however, rarely makes the news."

Waylon Perkins nodded in full agreement. "It seems to me that every young generation bucks the establishment. In my day, we called it 'the Man.' We were testing our limits, learning what we could get away with and what we couldn't, but overall, we weren't violent. My generation was more about sit-ins and peaceful protests. With each generation, it gets more aggressive, and more acceptable. A couple of years ago, people were tearing down every statue they saw, no matter who it honored or what it stood for. They were lashing out at anyone of authority, and the press glorified it. Some cities are going so far as to defund their police departments. It's created a feeling of hostility against the badge. And like with the statues, some people don't care what it stands for. A badge is a badge, and it stands for rules and authority, something they don't respect and don't adhere to."

"Well put, Chief Perkins," the sheriff said. "It's my suggestion that we all work together to pool whatever tips, information, and resources we have to find this person and bring them in, preferably before someone else gets hurt. Are we in agreement?"

"Absolutely," the Cougar Springs chief said.

"I think it's the only prudent thing to do," Brash concurred.

The Riverton chief was still unconvinced. "I think it's worth keeping in mind," he conceded, "but I'm not convinced these incidents are connect—"

Before he could finish, his phone rang. As he took the call, their police band radios went off simultaneously.

"Riverton SO to all departments. Officer down. Hit and run in Riverton. Injured is a forty-nine-year-old male. Repeat, officer down. Be on the lookout for a gray sedan, unknown make or model."

As dispatch called for an ambulance, Chief Manning sprang from his chair. "Excuse me. I have an officer down."

He rushed out the door, still refusing to acknowledge a connection between the attacks.

3

Madison still fretted over the call she received from her ambiguous caller. It was worrisome, to say the least.

"What has your heads in the clouds this afternoon?" her grandmother wanted to know. She sensed the distraction as soon as they took a booth at *New Beginnings* for their noon meal.

"Uhm, I'm sorry," Madison apologized, turning away from the window to look at Granny Bert. "You said something?"

"Where is your head today, girl?" the other woman asked. "I was asking what had you so distracted!"

"Oh." She had never been good at hiding the truth from the woman who had raised her, so she simply said, "A potential new client. I guess I was thinking about her call and not paying attention. What did I miss?"

"Not much," Bertha Cessna admitted. "Just an old lady grousing about being stood up by a friend."

Madison made a show of looking around their immediate area. "What old lady? I don't see any around here."

"Normally, I would agree. The calendar may say I'm

inching closer to eighty-four, but in my heart, I'm not half that. Lately, though, I have to admit to feeling the ticking of the clock."

This gloomy side of her grandmother definitely had her attention. Madison forgot all about her mystery caller and concentrated on her companion.

"Why do you say that? Have you not been feeling well lately? Do you need to see a doctor?"

"There's no cure for old age, girl. It's an honor you earn and, if you're lucky, it's something you'll die of."

"Lucky?" she asked skeptically.

"When you consider the alternative, absolutely!"

"I see your point. But this isn't like you to be so melancholy. Has something happened I don't know about?" Madison peered more closely at her grandmother.

"I reckon I'm just feeling a might bit sorry for myself. Like all things, it will pass."

The waitress brought their meal, and Madison smiled her appreciation. "Thanks, Dierra. This salad looks fantastic."

"I prefer the chicken and dumplings Granny Bert ordered, but both are good."

Related or not, almost everyone referred to the town's matriarch as 'Granny Bert.' It was a term of endearment, something that would normally lift her spirits. Her grandmother wasn't exactly what one would refer to as modest. She took pride in her standing in the community. She was a natural-born leader and authoritative figure, even when she didn't conform to authority or to what was widely deemed 'appropriate.' When labeled as outspoken, determined to push the limits, and downright nosy, the elderly woman took it as a compliment. She referred to her inquisitive nature as 'ferreting out valuable nuggets of information,' and sharing said nuggets (aka gossiping) as 'doling out useful knowledge and understanding.'

"Did anything in particular bring this on?" Madison asked once Dierra moved away.

"If you're asking who brought the meal, you're the one who needs to see a doctor!"

"Very funny. You know what I'm talking about. This unusual mood you're in."

"I suppose everyone has an off day now and then."

"Are you sure that's all this is?"

Granny Bert harrumphed. "Don't tell me you've decided to add psychological therapy to your list of services at *In a Pinch*."

Madison offered a superficially cheerful smile. "Nope. Just to people I know and love."

"I'll be okay, girl. Don't worry about me."

"I can't help it. I always worry about you." She softened her voice with a note of empathy. "Did you and Sticker have another falling out?"

"For Heaven's sake, I'm not a simpering teenager! My happiness doesn't revolve around a man, even a maddening one like that old coot. This has nothing to do with Sticker Pierce."

"I know your Bunco games aren't under attack anymore, and you just came back from another RV trip. Is it Uncle Jubal? I thought he was doing better now."

"It's not my brother, not my boys, not anyone in my family. Not my hobbies, either."

Madison sighed with frustration. "You're not making this easy, you know! Getting information out of you is like pulling teeth!"

"Then eat your rabbit food and quit asking so many questions."

"Isn't that like the pot calling the kettle black? You're one to be complaining about someone being nosy!"

"I never used the word nosy, but if it fits..."

"Okay, I'm being nosy. But only because I care. You're always a bit testy, but not like this." She anticipated the argument brewing and shut it down. "Oh, no you don't. Don't go off on a tangent about me calling you testy, because you know it's true, and because we both know it would just be a diversionary tactic to keep from answering my question!"

"After that long and exhausting speech," her grandmother sniffed, "I plumb forgot what the question was."

"No, you didn't." Madison stabbed at a piece of lettuce, aggravated when she missed. She kept stabbing, collecting a random stack of greens and carrots and cucumbers on the tines. "You know what? Just forget it. Forget I asked! Be gloomy if you want to. It fits my mood!"

"At least we're in agreement," Granny Bert said, slurping in the hot chicken broth.

After a moment of eating in silence, her previous words dawned on Madison. "Wait a minute. You said you were stood up by a friend? What friend?"

Her grandmother sighed. "This, again? I thought we were changing the subject."

"Yet we said nothing, so here we are again, back at the same subject. Who stood you up?"

"If you must know, Sybil. My best friend stood me up."

A memory tickled Madison's mind. "That's right, you two were planning a shopping trip into Houston. You were supposed to spend the night with her oldest son and his wife."

"That's right. But when I called to see what time we were leaving, she said she had decided not to go. She didn't bother to tell *me* that, though, and I already had my suitcase packed!"

"That's a little odd. Usually, Miss Sybil is more

thoughtful than that.”

“Not lately, she hasn’t been.”

“Is something going on with her? Is she not feeling well?” Madison was genuinely fond of her grandmother’s best friend since childhood, and she couldn’t help but worry about her, as well.

“I wouldn’t know,” Granny Bert snapped. “I hardly see her anymore. It seems she has better things to do than keep up with an eighty-year-old friendship.”

Madison fought back a knowing smile. Her grandmother was jealous because her friend wasn’t spending as much time with her as usual. It was cute, in a schoolgirl sort of way.

“What’s keeping her so busy?” she asked.

“If you ask me,” Granny Bert said, leaning in as she spoke in a confidential tone, “I think she’s seeing someone on the sly.”

“Miss Sybil? I’ve never known her to have a boyfriend.”

“Never has. Like my Joe, her Benny was one of a kind, and no one else could ever measure up. Sure, I pass time with Sticker, but I’ll never marry again. Sybil’s always said the same thing, but that doesn’t mean she’s changed her mind about stepping out with someone.”

“Of course not. She’s free to make her own decisions about that. But what makes you think she’s seeing someone?”

“She’s been going to that new spa a lot lately. She’s all into their lotions and oils, and she’s started wearing her hair different. After fifty years of wearing the same style, that’s saying something. And this isn’t the first time she’s changed our plans at the last minute. She leaves and won’t say where she’s been. True, she doesn’t owe me an explanation, but she’s told me about her goings-on for as long as I can remember. She’s just been acting different lately, and I think it's because she's seeing someone."

"Well, if she is, good for her. She deserves some happiness, the same way you do."

"Then why is she seeing him on the sly? Is she ashamed of him or something?"

"I know Miss Sybil isn't the kind of woman to be seeing a married man, so it must be something else."

"I suspect it's someone she doesn't think I'll approve of. Which is nonsense since we always support one another. Why, the only man around here I wouldn't approve of her seeing is Otis Perry! Some of the others don't deserve her, but I wouldn't object to her seeing them."

"Well, whoever it is, once she's ready to share who she's seeing, maybe the four of you can go on double dates."

"Not sure it's called dating at our age, but maybe we could play rummy or forty-two," Granny Bert grumbled.

They ate the rest of their meal and contemplated dessert. Granny Bert was in a slightly better mood, but she still seemed subdued.

Then again, so did Madison.

As Dierra delivered their coffee and Gennydoodle cookies, Granny Bert turned the tables on her granddaughter.

"Okay, you wheedled the truth out of me. Now it's my turn. Why the worried expression all through lunch?"

"I told you; I was thinking about a woman who called the office yesterday."

"I know what you told me. Now I want to know what's bothering you about it."

Again, she considered dodging the truth, but Granny Bert always saw through her. Besides, maybe she would have a clue as to who called. There was a saying around The Sisters: *'If Bertha Cessna don't know it, it ain't worth knowing.'* Her grandmother had an uncanny knack for knowing everyone and everything.

"I had a very strange call yesterday," Madison finally divulged. "A woman wanted to hire me to keep her from… doing something dangerous."

"Dangerous? What kind of dangerous?"

Madison looked around to make certain no one could overhear her words. "Murder dangerous."

As the mother of four boys, a former justice of the peace, and the former mayor of Juliet, Granny Bert had heard a lot of things in her eighty-three years on earth, but that statement took her by surprise. She sat back in her seat and let out a low whistle. "That is dangerous." After a moment of contemplation, she asked, "Who's the unlucky recipient of her wrath?"

"That's what's really confusing," Madison said, wiggling in her own seat. "I believe the woman is truly worried. She's afraid she's capable of following through with her threats. She says she feels this overwhelming rage come over her, and she's filled with hatred. I believe her when she says she's afraid of what she might do."

"Okay, but who is it? A cheating husband? His mistress? The banker who's calling in their mortgage?"

"She didn't say."

"So she's waiting to tell you who, until you've decided to take her on as a client," Granny Bert speculated. "I suppose that's smart. That way you can't call the police and turn her in if you don't know who her intended victim is."

"That's only half the problem."

"What's the other half?"

"She says even *she* doesn't know who it is she's

going to kill."

Her grandmother stared at her without blinking. "You're serious?"

"Yes. What's more, I think she is, too."

Granny Bert reached for a cookie and shrugged. "She sounds like a nutcase to me."

"But what if she isn't? What if she's serious, and I don't try to help? If she ends up killing someone, even hurting them, I'll feel awful. I think I'm compelled to try to help."

"Maybe letting Brash handle it would be the better choice."

"I can't do that. Not only does he have his hands full right now, but I also promised her I'd hear her out before contacting the police."

"Why would you do something like that?"

"I was trying to gain her trust. It was before she admitted she didn't know who it was she wanted to kill, but I thought if I promised her anonymity, she would talk to me more freely."

"I suppose that makes sense."

"Maybe you could help me track her down?" Madison asked with a hopeful note in her voice. "If I can find her, maybe I can help her. Maybe I can stop her from truly harming someone."

"Sure. Maybe it's someone I know. I have a wide circle of contacts, so even if I don't know her, maybe some of them do. What's her name?"

Madison squirmed in her seat again. "That other half of the story thing? It's not just that she doesn't know who she wants to kill."

"What else is there?"

"I don't know who she is, either. She hung up without giving me her name."

She had stumped her grandmother and left her speechless twice in one day. It was a new record.

"Let me get this straight," Granny Bert said at last. "A woman called and said she wanted to hire you."

"Right."

"She said she needs you to keep her from hurting someone. To be more specific, to keep from killing them."

"Right."

"But she doesn't know who it is she wants to kill."

"Right again."

"And you have no idea who she is, either."

"Correct."

Madison looked at her grandmother with a forlorn gaze. "It's hopeless, isn't it? I may as well forget the call ever happened."

"Don't you dare!" For the first time since they arrived, she saw a spark in her grandmother's eyes. The Granny Bert she knew and loved rubbed her hands together in anticipation. Her cackle was filled with glee.

"Hot-diggity, we've got us a new case!"

4

The challenge of a new 'case' was just the thing to boost her grandmother's spirits, but not necessarily Madison's.

Her grandmother didn't actually work for *In a Pinch.* Nor did any of her friends, although they would beg to differ. According to Granny Bert, she and her closest friends—Wanda Shanks, Virgie Adams, and Miss Sybil—offered invaluable insight to many of Madison's cases. They called themselves the senior division of the temp agency. Brash referred to them as her 'geriatric sidekicks.'

In actuality, the insight part was true. With well over three hundred years of living and experience between them, the four ladies knew more history and details about the two towns and their citizens than Madison could ever hope to find in a computer data base. It was the 'case' part they had wrong. (That and the working part since she never actually paid them. The most they got out of it was a week's vacation, a modest reward split between them, and a small salary from a client they took upon themselves to help.) Like most other people in town, they seemed to think Maddy took cases to investigate, rather than clients to help when their employees left them in a lurch.

While Granny Bert may have been enthusiastic about sniffing out the mysterious caller, Madison was more worried about what might happen if they didn't. Would the woman carry through with her threat? Would her victim's blood be on Madison's hands because she hadn't immediately agreed to help? Intellectually, Madison knew she wouldn't be responsible, but convincing her heart and her conscience was a different matter.

Before they left the restaurant, Granny Bert was already plotting her next steps.

"I'll talk to the girls. Make a subtle inquiry about noticing if anyone seems particularly hostile lately."

Subtlety wasn't one of her grandmother's strong points. For that matter, the 'girls' she referred to were all in their eighties. But if anyone could find out the impossible, it was Granny Bert, so Madison sat back and let her plot.

"Keep in mind," Madison reminded her, "this woman may not be from The Sisters. She could be from Riverton, or anywhere in the area, actually. I've had clients from as far away as Navasota, you know."

"I remember your stint with the upholstery business, and the infamous chair you brought home quite well," Granny Bert informed her.

"I was just pointing out that she could be from anywhere."

"I don't think so. I think she's local to the county, for sure, if not immediately within this community. She wouldn't trust you with such a delicate matter if she didn't feel some sort of connection with you."

Madison looked stunned. "You think I know her?"

"Not necessarily. But when people are from the same neck of the woods, we all tend to bond with them, even if we don't know them personally. It's the same way with people from the same alma mater or the same fraternity. You have no clue who they are, but you have a connection, and therefore a certain loyalty to them. This woman believed she could trust you, and that you would be loyal enough not to go directly to the police."

"What about my loyalty to my husband, who *is* the police?" Madison pointed out.

"Two different things. Personal and professional. No, mark my words. She's at least semi-local."

Her grandmother was probably right, but Madison wouldn't give her the satisfaction of saying so. Perhaps she would have if Granny Bert were still in her morose mood, but with the older woman's spirits and confidence restored, Madison saw no reason to bolster her flagrant lack of modesty.

"With any luck, the woman will call back and save us both a lot of bother," Madison said. "I'll let you know if she does."

"Either way," Granny Bert said, holding the door open for her granddaughter, "we've got this. I have confidence we'll find her."

"We have to. There's too much on the line for us to fail."

She hadn't confided the main reason she was so frightened. As of this morning, there had been three random attacks within River County's small boundaries. The minute Brash mentioned a firefighter had been shot, a cold fear had settled into Madison's heart. A deputy, a medic, and a fireman had all been targeted by one or more unknown assailants. All three victims were first responders. The same as Brash. What if this unknown caller happened to be the vile person committing these crimes? How could Madison possibly live with herself, knowing she may have had a chance to stop this monster before striking again?

While Madison fretted, Granny Bert had changed

conversation topics. "I'm dropping a casserole off to Sylvia Robles later this afternoon."

"Who?"

"Sylvia Robles. Her grandson was the firefighter killed this morning on the call to the Bates' gas station. I know Brash was the first on the scene."

"How do you know these things?" Madison asked in disbelief. "And how do you know his grandmother?"

"I've known Sylvia for years. She worked in the courthouse when I was a JP. I didn't know Jose, but I remember his father well."

"You literally do know everybody," Madison said, still dazed by her grandmother's seemingly endless connections.

"I also know that on record, officials are only saying he was killed in the line of duty, but what has Brash told you?"

"Why do I think you already know the answer to that question?" There was more than a hint of suspicion, perhaps even accusation, in her voice.

"Because I probably do. He was shot, wasn't he? It was a false alarm, the same way that stranded motorist call was falsified last week when Nancy Sloan was shot in the leg."

"I plead the fifth."

"Because you know I'm right!" Granny Bert said in triumph. "It was the same MO. I'm right, aren't I?"

"You know Brash has a strict policy about discussing ongoing investigations."

"Have it your way, missy, but we both know I hit the nail on the head." She opened her car door, calling over the top of her long, ancient Buick, "And tell Brash to keep his head down. He's a first responder, too."

Madison ran a few errands before coming home.

She was surprised to see that Brash was already there.

"Why are you home so early?" she asked as she saw him at the breakfast nook, nursing a cup of coffee. "Not that your middle of the night call doesn't necessitate it, but you're usually too stubborn to admit to being tired."

"Not this time," he said with unabashed candor. "Have a seat."

"Uh-oh. Why do I think I'm not going to like what you're about to say?"

"Because you're not going to like what I'm about to say."

Madison took time to put the milk and butter into the refrigerator before joining him at the table.

"What is it, Brash? What aren't I going to like?"

"Our lunch meeting was interrupted today when a call came in over the radio."

"Not another one!"

"I'm afraid so. This was a hit and run."

"What office this time?"

He looked surprised by her question. "Office?" he asked cautiously.

"It hasn't escaped my attention that all these attacks have been on first responders. Granny Bert has noticed it, too. So, what office?"

Brash grunted in reluctant admiration. "I'll give her one thing. She's a sharp ol' gal, even at her age." He took in a breath before releasing it on a long sigh. "Unfortunately, Riverton Chief of Police Manning is too blind to see what you and your grandmother have already picked up on, even when it was one of his own men who was injured."

"So, a police officer this time." Her voice was quiet.

"Yes. One you know, too. Detective Walt Leads."

"The one who gave me so much grief this summer?"

"One and the same."

"I'd like to say something snide, but the truth is, I hate to hear about anyone being hurt. Especially when they've been targeted by a maniac." She lifted her hazel eyes to his brown ones. "That's what's happening, isn't it? First responders are being targeted."

Brash reached out to take her hand. "Here I was dreading telling you, and my beautiful and intelligent wife beat me to the punch. I should have known you would figure that out, even without me. But yes, I do think that's what's happening. I think someone is targeting first responders."

"But why?" She was genuinely perplexed.

"It's the badge they hate."

"I know there's bad officers of the law. There's always that one exception to every rule, no matter what it is. But the vast majority are only out there to help. Don't people see that? You put your lives on the line every time you pin that badge on and step out the door. Why would someone hate you just because you choose to serve the public?"

"I can't answer that, sweetheart. Some things just can't be explained."

Madison pushed her hand through her hair. "Now what?" she asked.

"Now we catch the sorry SOB who's doing this."

"How? Do you have any evidence? Any witnesses?"

"Neither, I'm afraid. Not yet. But we will," Brash said with confidence. "And when we do, we'll make an arrest. And we'll make sure it sticks."

"I just hope it's in time to save someone else from getting hurt, or worse."

"Me, too, sweetheart."

"How is Leads, by the way?"

"He's banged up. Probably has one, if not two, broken legs. But he'll survive."

"And probably be meaner than ever," she muttered

beneath her breath.

"I heard that." He winked and admitted, "But you're probably right."

"Seriously, though, how do you plan to protect yourself? Not just you—although you are my top priority—but everyone who wears a badge?"

"That was part of our discussion today. Each department is putting out a memo to all personnel and holding mandatory briefings starting tomorrow morning. We'll urge everyone to be extra vigilant and to be aware of their surroundings at all times. No one will go on a call alone, no matter what office they're with. In fact, I've called a meeting for this evening, requesting all department heads to be there. Fire department, EMS, clinic, security teams, anyone who represents a badge of any sort."

"This is scary, Brash. And so hard to believe it's happening *here*, in our little close-knit community. For that matter, here in our River County. We're so small. Most of our towns and communities are connected in some way. More often than not, in multiple ways. It's hard to imagine there's a killer among us."

"I agree, but four attacks are just too much of a coincidence, no matter what Manning believes."

"I think I see a pattern among Riverton PD officers. They all have tunnel vision."

"Yep. He trains them to be just like him."

"What time is your meeting this evening?"

"Seven."

"I may see if Genny and the girls want to come over, since Cutter will be at the meeting. If it's too close to their bedtime, I may go there, instead."

"I think that's a good idea. The two of you don't get to spend much time together anymore, do you?"

"She owns a busy restaurant—Granny and I ate there today, by the way—and she's the mother of two one-year-olds. It's not like she doesn't have her hands full."

"You've been there. You know what it's like."

"Don't I, though? I was exhausted from five months before the twins were born until they were about ten years old. Then the teenage years set in, and it was a different kind of exhaustion. And now, with them both away at college…"

"You're exhausted from worrying about them," Brash said with a knowing smile. "I get it. I have the same problem."

"And I'm sure you're exhausted after last night. Why don't you go in the family room and relax? Maybe take a little nap before you have to go back in."

"I really should go to the station."

"You really should rest. Please? For me?"

He gave her a sexy smile. "I have a better idea. Why don't we both go upstairs and lie down?"

"Because then you wouldn't be sleeping."

"Sleeping is overrated."

Madison laughed. "At least try to take a power nap. Don't take this the wrong way, but you look like you could definitely use it."

"Hard to be insulted by the truth."

"I promise not to let you sleep too long. We'll have an early dinner so you can eat before the meeting. How's that sound?"

"Perfect, since I only ate half my lunch. I lost my appetite after listening to Manning's pompous attitude."

"Then go in there and relax. I insist."

Dropping a kiss onto his mouth, she sent him off for some much-needed rest.

5

"I've called everyone in this morning for a very important briefing," Brash said to his small crew of four deputies. Vina sat in, as well.

"As I'm sure you all are aware, there have been several random attacks in our county recently. The first took place ten miles outside Cougar Springs and involved a River County Deputy." He pushed a pin into the map mounted to a wall in their 'situation room.' They gave the space its nickname because it was used as the situation warranted. In some situations, it was a work room. In others, it was an interview room, or even a break room. In this situation, it was used as a meeting room.

"The second took place a week later on County Road 452, two miles out of Naomi, when one of The Sisters' emergency medical technicians was hit by a bullet from an unknown shooter." He pushed in another pin.

"The third was early yesterday morning, when a Riverton VFD firefighter took open fire between here and Indian Meadows. As a result, he was mortally injured and died at the scene." A third pin denoted the place. "Just after noon yesterday, a fourth attack took place in Riverton proper, when a hit and run driver struck and injured a detective with the Riverton PD." He added the fourth pin.

"As you can see, the attacks are taking place all over the county in no particular form or fashion. One was a direct blow to the head, two were discharged firearms, one was vehicular. The only common denominator is that all the victims were first responders. They all wore a badge, whether physically or metaphorically."

"What are you saying, Chief?" newly appointed Deputy Stone asked.

"I'm saying we are under attack. Us, and every one of our brothers and sisters in public service. All four of these attacks occurred after a false report of suspicious circumstances. A prowler, a stranded motorist, a smoke alarm, a fender bender. Each time emergency personnel arrived, they were ambushed and harmed. Or worse, in the case of Jose Robles."

"What can we do about it?" Misty Abraham wanted to know. "How can we protect ourselves and our fellow first responders?"

"Effective immediately, no one will respond to a call without a partner as back-up."

"How's that going to work?" Deputy Perry asked in protest. "There's only the four of us!"

"When have I ever failed to take my share of shifts, Otis?" Brash asked with the infamous arc of his eyebrow. The imperious look was more of a dare, known to make grown men cower and criminals confess to deeds they may or may not have done. He had used it as a professional ballplayer, college football coach, father, and now as an officer of the law.

"Five," the older officer amended. There was grudging respect in his voice, even though a hint of resentment lingered beneath the surface. Otis Perry had been on the force far longer than anyone and felt he should have been awarded the position of chief.

"Otis has a point, sir," Deputy Schimanski said in a more conciliatory manner. "How can the five of us double up and still provide adequate coverage for the community? Between the two towns, we cover a lot of territory. Even working round the clock, seven days a week, I don't see how that's going to work." He respectfully added, "Sir."

"Both of you are right. Doubling up won't work. That's why we're partnering with the fire department to see that both departments are adequately covered when responding to a call. Fire Chief Cutter Montgomery has promised the cooperation of his crew. Several attended a special meeting last night and signed up for twenty-four-hour on-call shifts. From this moment forward, a member of the fire department will accompany each of us when we're called out. In return, one of us will ride along on their calls. Vina will coordinate shifts."

"We can't ride with the fire department on every call and still do our jobs as officers of the law!" Otis Perry forcefully objected.

Brash considered the seasoned officer to be a good lawman. Brash gave Perry the respect he was due as both an elder and a fellow officer. He defended Perry when Madison, Genny, and Granny Bert aired their long-standing grievances over his abrasive personality. But Brash would allow no dissension within the department.

Without singling out Otis, his voice brooked no argument when Brash addressed the room. "This is not a request. Until further notice, we are joining forces with the fire department. If you don't sign up voluntarily for the days of your choice, Vina will assign shifts."

In a more relaxed manner, Brash pointed out to his team, "Look. We work together with the fire department on almost a weekly basis. They provide traffic control when we work an accident. We provide crowd control when they respond to a major fire. The only difference is that we'll be pairing with them on a coordinated schedule rather than on an as-needed basis. I realize it means mandatory on-call shifts. Fewer-to-no days off. But it's not permanent. It's a temporary measure until we can catch the maniac who's targeting our people. This is for all of our safety, and it's not optional."

Nate Stone raised his hand. "Do we have any leads, sir, as to the identity of this person?"

Brash's sigh carried throughout the room. "Unfortunately, no. So far, we have no eyewitnesses, no weapon, no prints, nothing. We don't even have definitive proof these attacks are related, but the similarities don't escape attention. All are erroneous distress calls, all are ambushes, all are on first responders."

"You've told us often enough," Abraham murmured, "that you don't believe in coincidence."

"Not when it comes to police work, I don't," he agreed. "Nothing like this has ever happened in River County before. Even if the attacks were on random individuals with absolutely nothing in common, it would be a compelling enough coincidence to warrant closer attention. We can't assume these are random and individual acts. Until we can prove otherwise, we have to investigate as if they are related."

"Are you saying we have a serial attacker among us?" To his credit, Nate's voice didn't waver when he voiced the disconcerting question.

Brash answered slowly, and with care. "I hesitate to use the word 'serial,' as it comes with heavy connotations. But yes, I do tend to think of this as a repeat offender, although I still reserve judgment on that assumption. This could be the work of more than one individual. I know none of us like to think of this in a small community like ours, but there's a possibility this could be the work of a gang. This could be an initiation challenge. I'm not saying we have an active and vicious gang infiltrating our county, but it's entirely possible."

Stone raised his hand again. "Is it possible this is the work of a gang in one of the bigger cities, who uses smaller communities to carry out their initiations? They might mistake us as lazy little departments who don't have the smarts or the manpower to find the perpetrators."

Brash's brown eyes glittered like granite. "And they would be wrong," he said in a voice just as hard.

He then visibly relaxed his tensed shoulders and said in a more conversational manner, "But you are absolutely right, Deputy Stone. They could travel to outlying areas, hoping to remain undetected and unhindered. With that in mind, be aware of anyone who appears out of place. Anyone showing open disdain for ordinances and laws, anyone who acts suspicious, anyone who seems to be overly interested or overly covert. While plenty of our own citizens fall into that pattern, it would be prudent to check them out. Run plates, inquire locally, be aware of what they do and where they go."

"Aren't you afraid someone will accuse us of profiling?" Perry growled, but his ire wasn't directed to his boss.

"I hardly consider watching for suspicious-looking characters as profiling. I'm not suggesting they be of a particular age, race, gender, religion, or anything specific. I'm referring to normal observation of anything noticeably different, be it people, vehicles, or situations. And if some highly opinionated someone does consider that profiling, I'd rather take heat over that than trying to explain why more innocent people have been killed."

"Are we ramping up patrol?" Schmanski wanted to know.

"Yes, to whatever extent that's possible. In case our perpetrator sees a window of opportunity and acts impulsively, I want patrol done in pairs, as well as calls."

"What do you mean by extent?"

"The fire department is strictly volunteer, so most have paying jobs they have to take into consideration. When possible, our department will cover routine patrol. For today, Abraham and Perry will be one team, Stone and Schmanski the other. I have meetings lined up but will be flexible enough to be on call for the fire department. Vina is working out a schedule that should make sense of it all." He flashed the woman a smile. "Lord knows if anyone can do it, it's Vina."

The radio squawked with a tone-out for The Sisters Fire Department. One of the other dispatchers answered the phone lines while Vina was in the meeting.

"I believe that's my cue," Brash said. "Remember, deputies. Be alert, be careful, be safe."

6

Madison worked on reports and let her only employee, Derron Mullins, handle the rest.

She had spent most of the morning taking another stab at locating her mysterious caller. The effort was wasted. The woman didn't pick up the phone, there was no traceable listing associated with the number, and she still had no clue who the caller might be.

Shortly after lunch, Derron answered with his perky spiel. "Good afternoon, you've reached *In a Pinch Professional Services*. This is Derron speaking. How may I be of assistance to you today?"

For the most part Madison tuned him out, until she realized he had spun in his chair and was looking at her. "Are you available to take a call?" he asked in a loud whisper.

"Do you know who it is?"

Derron shook his head. "She didn't say."

Her heart quickened. "Put her through," she instructed, reaching for her phone.

"Hello? This is Madison."

"It-It's me," the woman said simply.

Madison felt almost weak with relief. "I'm so glad you called back."

"I almost didn't."

"But you did, and that's good. That's very good."

"Who's there with you?" The woman turned suddenly suspicious. "Is that your husband?"

"No, that's my assistant, Derron Mullins."

"He didn't answer the phone the other day."

"If you knew Derron," Madison said dryly, unable to resist a small smile, "you'd understand when I say he'd gone shopping."

"Can he hear our conversation?"

"Only my side of it."

"If you told him to leave, how would I know he really did?" the woman asked cautiously.

Without answering directly, Madison held the phone away from her ear. "Derron, why don't you take the rest of the afternoon off?"

"Are you serious, dollface? Wait. Don't answer. You might change your mind!" The petite man didn't bother turning off his computer. He opened a drawer, took out his wallet, slammed the drawer shut, and left his chair spinning as he vacated the seat. "You're the best boss ever! Tootles," he called over his shoulder.

Madison returned to the phone. "Hear that slamming of the door? That was Derron, off for another round of shopping. His favorite boutique is having a sale."

"Oh."

The caller seemed at a loss for words, but that was understandable. Derron left a lot of people speechless.

"Like I said, I'm glad you called back. What were you saying the other day when we got cut off?" Madison tried to make light of the woman hanging up so abruptly.

"I told you I needed your help."

"Yes, that's right. But you didn't say exactly how I could do that. Can you tell me what you had in mind?"

"I don't know. That's why I want to hire you!" the woman said in exasperation.

"I want to help you. I do. But I'm sorry, I don't even know your name."

She was hesitant to answer, but at last Madison heard a faint, "Delphine. It's Delphine."

Madison pumped her arm in silent triumph. *Yes! She had a name!*

When she spoke, her voice was purely professional. "Delphine. What a lovely name. Okay, Delphine, you say you need help, and I want to help you. It's a good start, but I need to know more."

"Like... what?"

Despite hoping the woman would call back, Madison hadn't formulated a plan of any kind in case she did. She scrambled now for something to say.

"Well, normally when a client hires me, they tell me what the job is, when they want it done, that sort of thing. Let's start there."

"I, uh, I want you to keep me from doing something horrible. And I want you to start as soon as possible!"

"Good. That's a good start."

But, Madison lamented, *where did she go from here?* Normally, she would suggest they meet, but did she *really* feel safe meeting with the woman face to face? Delphine confessed to wanting to kill someone. True, she wasn't sure just who she wanted to kill, but what if anyone would do? Someone like *her,* for instance?

Madison gulped at the thought, then silently scolded herself. The woman was reaching out. She was asking for help, and Madison could very well be the only one able to do so. She couldn't turn her back on her.

It was best to just dive in. "Delphine," she said quickly, before she could change her mind, "I think we should meet.”

“Where?”

“Do you have a car?”

“Yes.”

Thinking about the car involved in the hit and run accident—Brash said it was a gray sedan—Madison left herself one more chance to opt out.

“Excellent. What color?”

“Red. But what does that—”

“So, I’ll know it’s you,” Madison explained hastily. “You can come here, to my office. Do you know where that is?”

“The old mansion everyone calls The Big House. Second and Main, in Juliet.”

“That’s right. My office is at the front right, with a big wrap around porch. There’s a side entrance for client parking.”

“Okay. I guess I can come.”

“Good. I think we need to talk.”

“Give me twenty minutes.”

“Of course. See you then.”

Madison immediately called her grandmother.

“She called back,” she blurted out, forgoing a greeting.

“Good, because I haven’t roused up a thing.”

“Her name is Delphine, she drives a red car, and she’ll be here in twenty minutes.”

“You got all that in a phone call? I’m impressed!” Granny Bert said. “See? I told you I’m rubbing off on you!”

“Any guess as to who she is?”

“Hmm. I’ll have to think about that. In the meantime, why don’t I sit in on the meeting?”

Madison was hesitant. “I don’t know. She didn’t want to talk with Derron here. I had to give him the rest of the day off, so she’d feel comfortable enough to talk to me, and that was just over the telephone."

"Did it occur to you that maybe she *wants* to get you alone? I'm definitely coming over!"

"You can't. I don't want to blow my chance at getting through to her. What if... what if *she's* the one committing these horrible crimes? If something happened to Brash or any of our friends in public service, I would never forgive myself."

"And I would never forgive myself if something happened to you. Your house doesn't have all those secret passages for no reason. I'll hide in the wall behind your office. Lord knows it's not the first time I've done it!"

"I don't know..."

"I do. You don't have to do a thing. Stay in your office and wait for her. Listen to what she has to say. I'll let myself in the kitchen entrance and go through the passage that way. If you need anything, just say the word, and I'll come busting through!"

"Well..." Madison waffled. Admittedly, the idea did hold some merit.

There would be some who said an almost-eighty-four-year-old woman wouldn't be much in the way of backup. Those people, obviously, didn't know her grandmother. Nor had they ever seen her brandish a gun. Even at her advanced age, Madison would entrust her life to Granny Bert any day.

"Okay, you can come," she decided. "Stay out of sight and don't make a sound. I don't want to scare her off."

"Me? You won't even know I'm there."

"I mean it, Granny."

"So do I. I'll come out when your meeting's over so we can plot our strategy."

Madison had to admit she was apprehensive about the meeting. It might not be her best idea ever, but she felt compelled to meet the woman and hear her out. Granny Bert would be there if anything went wrong.

Less than twenty minutes later, someone knocked at the office door. Madison smoothed down her blouse, took a deep breath, and forced a smile as she opened the door.

She wasn't sure what she had expected, but it certainly wasn't this woman. Delphine was a plump, pleasant-looking woman with gray curls and a nondescript outfit typical for a woman her age: sensible black shoes, below-the-knee gray skirt, pale pink top with matching cardigan, and a long string of pearls. The pearls weren't real but were a good imitation. She appeared to be in her late sixties or early seventies and looked too sweet to harm a mouse, much less a human being.

"Delphine?" Madison asked a bit uncertainly.

"Yes. Madison?"

"Yes. Please, come in."

She often invited clients to have a seat in the cozy sitting area nestled into the turret, but today, she guided her guest further into the room. The closer they were to the secret passage, the better her grandmother could hear. Madison indicated one of the wingback chairs flanking her desk before slipping into her own seat behind the ornate antique piece.

She decided a direct approach was needed. "I have to be honest with you, Delphine. Our conversation the other day was quite disturbing."

"And I have to be honest with you. I'm surprised you suggested we meet. I thought I'd surely frightened you away."

"Should I be frightened?"

Delphine started to answer, then seemed to think better of it. After a brief pause, she said, "I'm not sure. If I'm being honest, I've frightened myself. I don't understand what is happening to me.”

“Have you changed any medications lately?”

“No. I can’t think of a thing I’ve done differently recently, other than I’ve started taking vitamins. My doctor recommended a good multi-vitamin and a calcium supplement. I discovered a wide variety at *Miss Zuri’s Essentials*, right here in The Sisters.”

“Is this your general practitioner or a… specialist?” Madison wasn’t certain how to politely ask if she were seeing a psychiatrist.

“I know what you’re asking. No, I’m not seeing a shrink. He’s my family doctor.”

“And you’re in generally good health?”

“A little trouble with my gallbladder and keeping my cholesterol under control, but for the most part, yes. I always get a good report. And there’s nothing wrong with my mind, so that’s not the issue.”

“Then what is, Delphine?” she asked frankly. “You said you get this feeling of rage washing over you. Do you have trouble with your blood pressure? Anger issues?”

“My blood pressure has always been good. And normally, I’m a very easy-going person. I don’t get hysterical or overly dramatic. These episodes of anger have me completely baffled.”

“Have you discussed them with your doctor?”

“No. It’s… well, frankly, it’s embarrassing.”

“What about your family?”

“Oh, Lord, no! They would be horrified. Believe me, *I’m* horrified enough! I just don’t understand what’s happening.”

Madison did believe her. Delphine seemed to be a sweet, perfectly normal older woman.

“Short of suggesting you have your doctor perform a complete check-up, I don’t see how I can help you, Delphine.”

"You can keep me from doing something terrible, like killing someone!"

"How would I do that, Delphine?" Madison asked, not unkindly. "I can't keep you locked up."

"Maybe you should! Maybe that's exactly what you should do!"

"Not me, Delphine. Your doctor, perhaps, but not me."

"So, you *do* think I'm crazy!" She looked more disappointed than she did angry.

"I never said that. But how can I stop you from harming someone, if you don't even know who that someone is?"

Tears welled in the other woman's eyes. "I don't know. I don't know anything anymore, except that there are times when I get this overwhelming urge to just... to just tear into someone! I don't mean just slap them. I mean hurt them. Badly. Fatally."

The words weren't compatible with the heart-shaped lips saying them. Delphine seemed convinced they were true, but Madison wasn't sure *she* was.

"Tell me about some of those times. What were you doing when you felt the anger wash over you?"

"Well, let me see... Okay, once I was just sitting there in my recliner, watching that police drama with Tom Selleck. He's still so handsome, don't you think? And suddenly, I just got so angry, I was shaking! I was so mad, I took off my shoe and flung it at the screen! It didn't do any damage to the television, but my shoe bounced off of it, hit a potted plant, and dumped soil all over my living room rug!"

Madison bit back a smile at her dramatic play by play. "And what about the other times?"

"Well, one of the times I was getting a pedicure, and I was listening to some of the other ladies talking. I don't even remember the conversation, but I remember getting angry. *Very* angry. Angry enough that I made that poor little girl doing my toes cry. I wasn't even sure she understood English, but she understood I was mad as a hornet!"

Madison was positive Granny Bert was behind the wall laughing. It was hard enough for her to keep a straight face. This little lady didn't sound remotely like a killer.

"Another time, I know I was at a red light when the feeling came over me. It took all my self-control not to ram the car in front of me! I wanted to hurt something. Anything. Better yet, some*one*."

So maybe Madison was wrong. A sense of unease wiggled its way up her spine. "Were you by chance in Riverton midday yesterday?" she asked cautiously.

"No. I went with my sister-in-law to Bryan yesterday. That's where her cancer doctor is. Why do you ask?"

"Oh, no reason, really. I just know there was a hit and run accident there, and something you said made me think about it."

"My day was spent at doctor appointments, one of those all-you-can-eat buffets, and WalMart."

"Back to those fits of anger you feel. Were there any more episodes you recall?"

"A few."

"Can you tell me about them? What you were doing at the time, what you felt, anything at all?"

"I know how I felt. I felt furious. Absolutely furious. The kind of furious where you want to throw things, slam things down, kick, scream, bite. I've never done any of those things, mind you, but when that feeling washes over me, I know I can do every one of them and more."

"More?"

"Like I told you over the phone. When that feeling

hits me, I don't just want to hurt someone. I want to *kill* someone."

"Does… does that mean just anyone? I mean, if your sister were in the room, would she be in danger?"

"No! Of course not! I didn't kill the women at the spa, did I? Or the person in front of me at the red light? So far, the only thing I've actually killed is my English ivy plant, but I still have hope it will pull through."

"Then I think you've answered your own concerns, Delphine. You aren't as dangerous as you seem to believe."

The older woman looked confused and not entirely convinced. "I—I'm not so sure about that. My rage seems to be focused on *someone*; I just haven't crossed paths with them yet."

"Why do you say that?"

"Instinct?" She didn't seem sure of her answer.

"Are you asking me?"

"I don't know. That's just it! I. Don't. Know." Delphine wrung her hands in distress. "I don't know anything anymore."

Madison felt bad for the other woman. Delphine truly believed she was dangerous. She was worried she might hurt—or kill— someone. Madison didn't dare make light of her worries, but she couldn't quite buy into them, either.

"I think maybe you should talk to someone more qualified than I am, Delphine. I would truly like to help you, but I just don't know how. Frankly, you don't seem dangerous to me. You seem like a very nice person. But I know something is going on that makes you think differently, and I encourage you to find out, if for no other reason than your own peace of mind."

Delphine looked dejected. "I was hoping there was something you could do. I've heard so many people say you've solved all their problems. I thought maybe… I hoped..."

Madison chewed her bottom lip before caving with guilt. "Look. Maybe I can help somehow. What if you call me when you feel the rage taking over, and I help talk you through it? Do you think that might help?"

"I—I don't know. Maybe."

"It wouldn't hurt to try, would it?"

"I suppose not."

"Then let's do that. If either of us comes up with a better plan, we can try it, too, but I think this will be a good start."

Delphine looked relieved. "Yes. It's a good start. Thank you, Madison. Thank you so much!"

"I really haven't done anything yet."

"You listened. You didn't think I was crazy. That helps, truly it does." For the first time since her arrival, Delphine smiled.

When she was gone, Granny Bert came out from behind the hidden panel.

"So? What do you think?" Madison asked.

Her grandmother scoffed. "That woman is no more a killer than Sybil is!"

"I agree. There were times when I could hardly keep a straight face."

"Like when she missed her TV but killed her English ivy?" Granny Bert slapped her knee with a good, hearty laugh.

"Oh, she and her hornets are holding out hope it will pull through," Madison said with twinkling eyes. That sent them both into another round of laughter.

They finally sobered. "I don't know why she believes she could do such a thing," Madison said in all seriousness, "but I have no doubt she truly believes she wants to kill someone."

Granny Bert nodded her gray head. "Like I said, that would be about like Sybil killing someone.

Impossible." She clucked her tongue. "Well, I reckon now it's up to us to convince her otherwise."

7

After being on-call with the fire department and taking his rotation on patrol the next day, Brash was more than ready to crash the following evening. He ate and went straight to bed, only to be awakened before ten that night.

"I have a lead!" Otis Perry announced through the phone.

"A lead?" For one foggy moment, Brash had trouble remembering what case they were working. The fog cleared within a second, and he asked, "What it is?"

"I drew the short straw and had to ride with the fire department. Someone called in reports of smoke over near Sawyer Road. En route, I noticed two guys walking down the side of the road. They both had shaggy-looking hair, tattoos all over their arms and necks, and jeans with holes in them."

"Those jeans probably cost three times as much as my Wranglers," Brash broke in to mention.

"You're kidding me. They had rips and holes all through them!"

"Did you call to talk about jeans? If so, I'm going back to bed."

"I'm calling because the guys looked suspicious.

The smoke was coming from a barbecue pit, so we turned around and headed back to the station. We took a different route, and guess who we saw on County Road 451? Same two guys. They were in an older model Ford car. I ran the plates, and they were from a car reported stolen in Anderson County. I went back out to find them, but they were nowhere to be seen. Then—"

"Who rode with you?" Brash asked.

"No one. But listen, that's not—"

"No, Otis, you listen. I made it very clear that no one is to ride alone. If you don't have a partner, you don't go. Period." Brash was exhausted and in no mood to argue.

"But it was a hot lead! And you haven't heard the best part yet. These same two jokers were spotted over near Indian Meadows. I called Constable Lewallen, and he confirmed the car had been spotted at the gas station the night before Robles was killed. I think it may be enough to bring them in, boss. It's just a matter of who finds them first, us or them."

"It won't be you," Brash said tersely. "I'm having Vina reassign you to on-call fire duty again tomorrow."

"You can't do that!" the other man protested.

"I can, and I will. You disobeyed a direct order. Those orders are in place to protect you and the rest of our team. Until you can understand that, you're off patrol." Brash hung up without further ado.

It was a long while before he fell back to sleep.

"It was a stupid thing to do," Deputy Abraham agreed with her boss, "but Perry has good instincts. Maybe these guys are worth pursuing."

Brash looked over at his partner for the day. "You heard his description. Long hair, tattoos, ripped jeans. That's no help. Not when half of the male population between fifteen and twenty-five fit that description."

"But most of them aren't driving a stolen car."

"We don't know that these fellas are, either. He said the plates were off a stolen Chevy Bronco—the original, not today's version. This was an old Ford Grenada. No proof these guys switched the plates."

"You're right, but it's worth a shot. Especially if they were seen at the gas station the night before," Misty Abraham argued. "They could have been casing it."

"That's true, and the sheriff put out a BOLO to all departments. If we see the car or the men in our jurisdiction, we'll pursue them. But we're not going out of our way to look for them. We have our hands full as it is."

Abraham was quiet for a while as they drove a twisting network of intersecting county roads, alert to anything out of the ordinary. "Who do you think it is?" she mused after a while. "Who would do something like this?"

"Someone with an agenda, that's for sure," he said.

"Are you thinking one person or a group?"

"I don't know yet. I think we should be open to all possibilities."

"The attacks are different— blunt object, gun, car— but yet the same: all bogus distress calls. I'm thinking it's one person."

"You could be right."

"But you don't think so." There was a hint of disappointment in her voice.

"I didn't say that. I'm saying that at this point, we don't have sufficient evidence to sway my opinion one way or another. We should be open to all possibilities."

They drove in silence for several miles, until Brash spotted something up ahead. "What's that?"

"What?" She followed the path of his finger, squinting to see what he saw. "Oh. Uhm, it looks like a stranded motorist." There was trepidation in her voice.

"I'll call it in. Pull up behind them, but not too close. I'll see what's going on. Under no circumstances do you get out of the car unless I specifically say so. Got it?"

"But—"

"Got it?" he repeated in a commanding voice.

"Got it," she mumbled.

He arched his eyebrow in the way only he could do.

"Got it, *sir*," she amended.

"Stay alert. I can only see one person from here, but there could be someone else. Watch the perimeters. Keep the doors locked, the windows up, and the radio on standby." Brash tucked his back-up weapon into the leg of his cowboy boot and gave her a hard look. "This is *exactly* why I was so hard on Perry. This could be an ambush, and one of us needs to be able to call for help."

"If I see something suspicious, or someone sneaking up, I'll honk the horn."

"The radio will be more effective," Brash said with a small smile. "I have it turned low, and it's right here." He indicated the radio clipped near his collar bone.

As he opened the door, his deputy called out a worried, "Be careful!"

Brash approached the driver's side with care, noting a thirty-something woman behind the wheel. A child's car seat was buckled in the back seat, but he saw no evidence of anyone else with her, not even a child.

He tapped on the window lightly, motioning for the woman with vivid red hair to roll down the window. She looked aggravated.

"Yes?" she asked in a terse voice, rolling it down only halfway. She wasn't someone he recognized.

"Chief of Police Brash deCordova, ma'am. Are you having car trouble?"

"My battery's dead, if that's what you mean."

"Yes, ma'am, it is. I do believe that constitutes as

trouble." He kept his voice amiable, noting how agitated she seemed. It was possible she was nervous, but he sensed there was more to it.

"You're not going to give me a ticket, are you? Give me a lecture on how irresponsible I am to be caught out in the middle of nowhere with an empty charge? Preach to me about having an electric car?"

"It never crossed my mind to do any of those, ma'am," he replied pleasantly. "Do you have roadside assistance? Or sent someone to bring back a generator?"

Her eyes turned wary, and she leaned away from the window as far as her seatbelt allowed. "Why? Are you planning to do something to me if you think I'm alone?"

Her defensiveness put him on alert. "*Are* you alone, ma'am?" He inconspicuously scanned the trees in the distance.

"That's none of your business!" she snapped.

Brash sighed. It was too early in the day for such foolishness. "Ma'am, I need to see your driver's license and proof of insurance. You don't have to get out of the car. Just hand them through the window so I can call them in."

"You're giving me a ticket?" she screeched. "For having a stupid electric car with no battery charge?"

"No, ma'am, I'm just verifying your identity."

"I didn't give it to you."

At her smug tone, Brash nodded. "That's why I'm asking for your driver's license."

"It's Lauri. My name is Lauri."

"Good. Now I need to verify it by seeing your license." He held out his hand, palm up.

With a huff, Lauri dug into her purse and pulled out her wallet. "This is outrageous!" she complained. "All I did was run out of battery, and you're treating me like a criminal!"

"I'm doing no such thing—" he glanced down at the reluctantly proffered driver's license "—Ms. Lauri Beaver. I see here that you're from Cougar Springs. Is this still your current address?"

"Yes, and that's *Mrs.!*" she snapped. "Just wait until my husband hears about this!"

"Hears about what, Mrs. Beaver?"

"The way you're treating me. This is harassment!"

Brash didn't rise to the bait. "I'll just be a second, ma'am. Wait here, please."

The woman huffed her disdain. "I told you, my battery is dead. I don't have a choice but to wait."

Brash went back to the patrol car, reading the information into his mic as he walked.

"What is her problem?" Misty hissed when he opened the door. "We stopped to help, not to harass her."

"Don't talk too loudly. I want her to think I'm alone. She'll think I'm talking to dispatch."

"Why do you want her to think you're alone?"

"Just humor me," was all he said. While he waited for the report to come back, he called Rudy's Gas Station.

"Sorry, Brash, I don't do that. I sell gas, not 'lectricity," the old man said.

"Okay, I thought it was worth a shot, anyway. I'll call the fire department. They have generators on the trucks."

"You be careful out there, Brash. It's a crazy world we live in."

"You're not telling me anything I don't already know, but thanks. I appreciate your concern."

When Lauri Beaver's ID came back clean, Brash instructed Misty to call the fire department while he returned to the motorist.

Returning her license through the half-opened window, Brash said, "Okay, Mrs. Beaver, I've called for the fire department to bring their generator. They'll give you enough charge to make it home."

"The fire department! Why would you do that!" It was an accusation, not a question.

"Unless you have a roadside service provider and have already called them, the VFD is your best and fastest option. Cheaper, too," he added with a grin.

"Are you implying I can't pay? Because I assure you, I can!"

"They're a volunteer organization, ma'am, but I'm sure they would appreciate a donation if you're so inclined."

"Well, I'm not. And I'm not inclined to *tip* you, either!"

"I'm an officer of the law. I don't accept tips."

"Just bribes!" she spat.

Brash's eyes narrowed. "Ma'am, do you consent to taking a sobriety test?"

"What? Of course, I don't! You could change the results and give me a DUI. I refuse to take one. And why, I ask, would you even think I needed one?"

"You seem unnaturally belligerent, ma'am. I stopped to offer my assistance, and you've made a number of offensive accusations against me. I don't understand your anger unless it is induced by drugs or alcohol."

The irate woman clenched her fist, and Brash saw a flash of metal. His hand went to his service belt, resting atop his gun. "What's in your hand?"

"It's none of your business!"

"I think otherwise. Show me what's in your hand or step out of the vehicle."

She hesitated, seeming to weigh each option. After a moment, she unfurled her fingers.

"It's a nail file," she sneered. *"Satisfied?"*

"I will be when you hand it over." Seeing the calculating look in her eyes, he added, "Just like a knife or pair of scissors, with the pointed tip facing you."

"Are you planning to stab me?" she cried. Her fear appeared real.

"No, but I'm not planning on being stabbed, either." His tone allowed no argument. "Hand me the file, Mrs. Beaver."

Once she had relinquished the file with trembling hands, Brash's voice softened. "Mrs. Beaver, can you call someone you trust and put me on speakerphone? Your husband, perhaps?"

She looked suspicious. "Wh-Why?"

"I think you could use the reassurance, and I'd like to help you."

Clearly uncertain, she put her phone on speakerphone and hit redial.

"Donny? It's me. I have someone here who wants to talk to you." Just before she tilted the phone toward Brash, she said in a rushed voice, "It's a police officer! Don't trust him. He's trying to arrest me. I'm afraid he'll hurt me!"

"What?" the man called in alarm.

Brash spoke over them both. "Sir, this is Chief of Police Brash deCordova with The Sisters Police Department. I'm here with Lauri Beavers. Is that you're wife?"

"Yes! What's wrong? Has there been an accident? Why are you arresting her? Why are trying to hurt my wife?"

"I'm trying to help her. Nothing's wrong, other than the charge is dead on her EV. She's stranded on the side of the road, and I stopped to help, but she's suspicious of my intentions. I thought it would help if she could speak with you."

"Don't believe him, Donny!" Lauri yelled.

"Put me on FaceTime," Brash ordered. "That way he can see that I'm trying to help, not cause you harm."

Lauri did as she was told, but she still insisted, "He's lying, Donny. He's accused me of being drunk. Or high. He's harassing me!"

"Mr. Beaver, I only have your wife's best interests at heart. She's obviously very upset. I understand her frustration of being stranded on the side of the road, but I can assure you, I mean her no harm. I've called for the fire department to bring a generator and give her car enough charge to make it home safely. I intend to stay with her to ensure her safety, but she's not making it easy. I requested a sobriety test, which she was free to refuse and did, because I thought it might explain her belligerent behavior."

"Lauri? Belligerent? You must be mistaken!" her husband insisted.

"She hasn't been cooperative and is accusing me of misconduct. Is this normal behavior for your wife, sir?"

"Of course not! Lauri's the sweetest woman I've ever met!"

"You may want to head this way and be with your wife, sir," Brash suggested gently. "I think she needs you."

"Lauri! Lauri, what's wrong, sweetheart? What's happening? Why are you so upset?" The camera's view skewed as he pushed back from his desk and quickly stood.

Hearing her husband's concern, Lauri Beaver burst into tears. "I-I don't know what's wrong with me! I just got so angry. I-I thought..." She turned toward Brash, speaking to both men at once. "I'm so sorry, officer. I don't know what got into me. You're trying to help, and I... oh, hurry, Donny! Hurry, before I do something we'll all regret!"

8

Carrying a box into the post office, Madison found herself misty eyed. It was her weekly 'care package' to Blake, and it was filled with a few packaged snacks, a new bundle of socks, a belt he asked her to send, and a special treat from Genny: her signature Gennydoodle cookies, which he adored. Her son wasn't that far away in Waco, but he wasn't able to come home as often as Bethani did. Attending Baylor University on a baseball scholarship, his schedule was packed. Between practices, studies, and a part-time job on campus, it was difficult to make the hour-plus drive to The Sisters, even on weekends.

Enrolled at Texas A&M University, his twin usually came home every other weekend. It, too, was about an hour away, but in the opposite direction. Madison found it amusing that of the two, Bethani—who had adamantly objected to their move to Juliet and originally scorned all things 'country'—was the one to return the most often. Blake, on the other hand, had fallen in love with life in a small town. He missed being unable to roam at will over the deCordova Ranch, riding horses, fishing, and gathering for impromptu 'snackfests' with his friends. Madison found it ironic that he came home only on occasion.

Without the twins and all their friends, the rambling old mansion felt empty with only Madison and Brash there. At least they still had Megan home on a regular basis, especially now that she had a potential new boyfriend in town. Not that Madison cared about the reason. Her stepdaughter's vibrant personality made any space livelier. She still split time between the deCordova and Aikman households, but she made a point to visit both sets of parents each time she was home. And instead of mailing care packages to the girls, she simply handed them to Megan when she left.

Now, having mailed Blake's package, Madison swiped away the remnants of her last tear as her telephone rang. She fished the device from her purse and saw Delphine's name on her screen.

Hoping to sound cheerful, she greeted her caller. "Hello, Delphine," she said. She was afraid the woman on the other end was still skittish.

"Madison! I need your help!" Instead of sounding skittish, the older woman sounded frantic. "I-I have that feeling again! I'm practically seeing red!"

"Okay, okay. Don't panic." Madison had to give herself the same advice. "Where you are?"

"Shopping. Commerce Street in Naomi."

"What store are you in?"

"I was getting into my car when the rage hit me. I'm still sitting here." She hesitated before admitting, "I'm afraid to leave. I'm afraid of what I might do."

"Okay, good. Just sit there and relax for a moment. What store were you shopping in?"

"Well, let me see…" She took her time in answering. There weren't many stores in the town as a whole, much less on one street, so the pause seemed excessive. "First, I dropped in at *Miss Zuri's Essentials* for a tin of her special tea. It's the most divine mixture, something she blends herself, and it has such a unique taste. I asked what flavor it is, but she's very secretive with her recipe. I think she's afraid someone else will copy it if she reveals her secret ingredient. Whatever it is, I find that it's very calming, something I definitely need right now."

Madison listened to her ramble, knowing that the longer she kept Delphine on the phone, the less time she had to act on her rage. Barring there was no train coming through, Madison could be across the tracks and in Naomi in less than four minutes. She was already headed that way.

"I was already next door to *Tammy's Treasures*, so I decided to look for a gift for my niece. I didn't find anything that suited me, so I went down three doors to The Gift Co-Op. It's such a shame that those two buildings are empty in between them, right there on the main street in town, isn't it? I remember there was a shoe repair shop there years ago."

Madison let her rattle on, hoping it would defuse her anger. By the time Delphine had finished her trip down memory lane and detailed this morning's movements, Madison had the red car within her sights. She pulled into a parking space on the other side of the street so that she wouldn't be seen.

Finished with her long speech, Delphine said, "You've been a big help to me, Madison. I feel calmer now."

"I didn't really do anything."

"You listened, and you let me talk through my anger. It's gone now, as quickly as it came on." Frustration built in her voice as she added, "For the life of me, I can't imagine why this is happening to me!"

"I wish I had the answer, but at least the feeling has passed, and you can feel encouraged by the fact that nothing bad happened."

"That's true. Well, thank you again. Be sure and keep up with how many times I call you and how long I keep you on the phone. I intend to pay you for everything you're doing for me."

Madison didn't repeat that she had done nothing but listen. If it helped to reassure the other woman, she wouldn't spoil the moment.

Out of curiosity, Madison followed behind the red car as it backed out of the parking space. She kept a safe distance between them so Delphine wouldn't realize she was being followed. After a few turns, the red car pulled up at a modest house on North River Oaks. Madison idled at the corner, watching as Delphine used a key to let herself inside.

Not for the first time, Madison acknowledged that she had made a series of mistakes where Delphine was concerned. That first day, she had failed to get a name or any identifying information. Even when Delphine came to the office, she hadn't given her last name or address. The best she had done was offer her phone number. Which, Madison noticed, wasn't the same one she had called from before. That was another piece of information she needed to uncover, especially if it helped to explain Delphine's erratic behavior.

But she had an address now, and with it, she could get a last name and, hopefully, more information on her strange new client.

It was a start.

"Okay. I think I know who she is now." Granny Bert nodded her gray head when Madison dropped by to share the information. "Her maiden name was Bazajou. The family moved back to Louisiana when she was in high school, and I plumb forgot about her. That house on North River Oaks belonged to her aunt. She died about two years ago, so I guess Delphine either bought it or inherited it and decided to come back to Naomi."

"I'm not sure of her married name, but I have no doubt you'll find out." Madison smiled as she lifted the tea glass to her lips.

"I'm ashamed that I didn't already know these things. I must be falling down on my job." Granny Bert shook her head in disgust at her own shortcomings.

"You can't be expected to know every single person in both Naomi and Juliet. People are moving in and out all the time."

In response, her grandmother gave her a withering stare. Madison shrank back, sorry she had said anything.

Within minutes, Granny Bert made two phone calls, asked a few questions, and hung up with a satisfied smile. "It's not as bad as I thought," she reported. "Delphine's only been back about six weeks, and she's been so busy getting the house in order, she hasn't been out and about much. Apparently, the house was in bad shape and had quite a bit of junk inside."

"See? You aren't falling down on your job, after all." Not that gossiping and 'gathering information' was an actual job. "What else did you find out about her?"

"Her married name is Craddock, and she's a widow. She lived in Palestine for most of her married life, and her grandson came down to get her settled in. From what my sources tell me, she's sweet and mild mannered. No mention of mental illness or bouts of anger."

Madison smiled at the reference to 'her sources.' Sometimes, she thought her grandmother truly thought of herself as some sort of reporter. If she had a newspaper column, she should call it The Grapevine Curator. Or perhaps the Nuggets of Information Public

Service Announcement.

Abandoning the thought, Madison mused aloud, "Maybe the move has been traumatic for her. If she lived in one place for forty or fifty years, I'm sure it was hard for her to pick up her life and move to a new town. She may have lived here a long time ago, but a lot has changed since then."

"Maybe she didn't move on her own accord," Granny Bert agreed. "Maybe she was forced to leave her old house and had nowhere else to go."

Madison could definitely empathize. "I know that feeling all too well." When Gray died in a car crash and left her a widow, he also left her deep in debt. At thirty-nine with two teenagers to raise, her only choice had been to sell their house at a loss and move back here to The Sisters and live with her grandmother.

"She must have at least one child if she has a grandson," Granny Bert reasoned. "But who knows if she gets along with his parents? Or maybe they're missionaries like your father and live in Africa. If she had to leave her home, it may have left her mind temporarily unbalanced."

Madison picked up the thread of speculation. "The anger could be directed at the situation and not at a person."

"That should make her feel better about herself and ease her worries."

"I still think she should see a doctor. A medical professional could give her something for depression."

"Or introduce her to Wanda. Even as flamboyant as she normally is, I swear that woman's on some sort of mood booster these days!"

Madison's eyes widened. For the already unrestrained Wanda Shanks, that was a scary thought. "Please tell me she didn't have a professional margarita machine installed at her house." Granny Bert's friend was known to have a problem holding her liquor, not to mention her 'medicinal' marijuana.

"Lord, I hope not! No, this new mood she's in doesn't seem to be alcohol induced."

"Maybe she's got a fella, the same way Miss Sybil does. Have the two of them been going to the honkytonks without you?"

"Not that I know of. And, believe me, if Wanda had a new man friend, she wouldn't be able to keep it quiet. Remember her online 'romance' with the person she thought was Vartan Roosevelt?"

"I'd rather forget that entire fiasco," Madison said. She gladly changed the subject. "Any clues as to who Miss Sybil might be seeing?"

"None. Unlike Wanda, she's able to keep a secret if need be."

"With Miss Wanda, you never know what may be contributing to her new blast of enthusiasm. I swear," Madison smiled, "that woman may be in her eighties, but she acts more like a child. She gets a kick out of the simplest things."

"If you think she was enthusiastic before, you should see her new super-sized version of enthusiasm," Granny Bert complained. "She has the energy of a teenager and the attention span of a toddler."

"I hate to point this out, but the attention span thing isn't new."

"That's true enough, but there's something downright strange about the way she's been acting lately. And when I say Wanda Shanks is acting strange, you know it's *seriously* strange!"

"Hmm. You have a point." Madison's phone binged with a message. After reading it, she tucked the phone away and rolled her eyes. "Derron has some sort of 'emergency' at the office and needs me there. He probably has a paper cut or remembered there's another sale at some shoe store."

"Say, he's Wanda's roomie. Maybe he knows what kind of happy juice she's been drinking lately."

"That is a thought," she agreed, pushing in her chair as she stood. "I'll ask him as soon as he calms down from this latest crisis, whatever it might be." Her employee rented a room from Granny Bert's friend. Despite the age gap, they made perfect housemates for one another. Both were dramatic and unconventional.

Granny Bert followed her to the door. "I'll gather more intel on Delphine Craddock and let you know what I find."

"Thanks. Anything we learn will be more than we know. And at this point, we know next to nothing."

"We know she thinks she's dangerous."

"But I know that *I* find that hard to believe."

"I'll keep digging," her grandmother promised.

9

For once, Derron's idea of an emergency almost matched the definition used among the greater public.

Except that it wasn't exactly an emergency, and it wasn't exactly his.

But it came close on all accounts.

"What's wrong?" Madison asked when she arrived back at the office. She looked around, finding everything normal on the surface. "Where's the fire?"

"There's not a fire. Quite the opposite, actually."

Irritation flashed in her voice. "If it's an emergency, do we really have time for talking in riddles?"

"It's more like a flood," he clarified.

"We had a pipe burst? Where? Why didn't you say so?" Madison asked, rushing over to the coffee bar tucked into a corner of the office. Before she could examine the plumbing, Derron corrected her assumption.

"Not here. At home."

"Your home, or some other part of the house?" She twirled her finger to indicate the rest of the mansion beyond these walls.

"My home. Or Wanda's, to be technical, even though she's always telling me to consider it mine, too."

"Derron," she said, exasperated. "You insisted I rush home because we had an emergency."

"We do. I need you to come with me."

"Why? Can't you just call a plumber?"

"Not exactly. Come on, I'll explain in the car."

"Explain now."

"But this is urgent! Wanda needs us *right now*."

Madison agreed reluctantly. "Very well." She sighed as she followed him outside.

They crawled into the sports car Derron had 'gifted himself' on his last birthday. Independently wealthy, the younger man chose to work for Madison as a means of entertaining himself. Madison chose to keep him on because he was very good at his job, drama and all.

"Miss Sybil called and told Wanda she was bringing her a surprise," he explained as he shifted into gear, "but when she got there, Wanda didn't answer the door. Her phone went to voicemail, which was strange because her car was there, and they'd only hung up a few minutes before."

"What's strange is that for this to be an emergency, you're telling me a lot of useless information!" Madison snapped.

"Not useless," he insisted. "Explanatory."

"So, explain."

"Miss Sybil thought she heard Wanda calling her name, so she walked around the house so she could see where the voice was coming from. She narrowed it down to the bathroom on Wanda's side of the house. Thank the sweet Lord it wasn't my bathroom, because I just bought the yummiest little bathmat you've ever seen. It feels like—"

"Derron! The emergency?" As usual, he wasn't focusing.

"Oh, right. I'll tell you about the bathmat later. Anyhoo, Miss Sybil found the hidden key... Lord knows, it's not really hidden. I keep telling Wanda it's too obvious, but the old dear just won't listen."

"Neither will you," Madison ground out between clenched teeth. "Tell me what the so-called emergency is or take me back. This instant."

"Okay, okay." He rolled his eyes in a dramatic fashion. "Geesh. You won't even let a guy tell his story. So, Miss Sybil let herself in, and she found Wanda in the bathroom. Apparently, she was giving Lucky Ducky a bath in the sink. She couldn't get the sink faucet to shut off and water was going everywhere. In the process—"

Alarmed, Madison sucked in her breath. "Is she okay? Did she slip? Did Miss Sybil call the ambulance?"

"No, no, it's nothing like that. Well, sort of, but not really. When she couldn't make the water shut off, she put her finger in the spout, and it got stuck."

Madison stared at the man behind the steering wheel. "Let me get this straight. She got her finger stuck?" she asked in a dangerously quiet voice. "*That's* what this emergency is about?"

"Yes! Her finger is stuck, and they can't get it free! It's starting to swell and turn blue. She's lost circulation in it."

"Then they should call a plumber. Or the paramedics. Or both. But not *us*! What good are we going to do?"

"She can't call a plumber. Or an ambulance."

"Maybe she can't, but Miss Sybil certainly can."

By that time, they had reached the house and Derron was already out of the car. Madison had trouble keeping up with him as he ran inside, calling his roommate's name.

"Back here!" Miss Sybil called out.

"Don't you dare come in!" Wanda warned. "Send Madison in."

The door was closed, but they could hear Lucky Ducky, Wanda's 'support' duck, quacking in protest.

"Why me?" Madison asked, hand poised on the doorknob.

"Didn't I tell you?" he said, all but pushing her inside. "Wanda doesn't have any clothes on!"

Of all the things Madison could live her entire life without ever seeing, a naked Wanda Shanks was near the top of the list.

Time, nor gravity, had been kind to the woman. Skin stretched, puckered, and sagged in places Madison never dreamed of. Wrinkles disappeared into rolls of fat and seemed to come out on the other side, still a saggy testament to time and a penchant for sweets.

"Sweet Jesus, am I happy to see you!" Miss Sybil cried with relief. "Her finger is swelling, there's no getting it out, and the rest of the pipes are about to blow! We need to get her dressed so we can call for help."

As the water pressure built, tiny fissures were appearing at all the pipe joints. Water trickled along every seam, threatening to make Sybil's words true.

"Did you turn off the valve?" Madison ducked under the sink and found the valve to shut off the water. She backed out without turning her head, carefully avoiding another unpleasant sight up close and personal.

"Oh, lordly, I didn't even think of that!" Sybil groaned.

"Neither did I!" Wanda said, laughing hysterically. "Oh, Sybil, where were our heads?"

"I don't know about you, but I was busy trying to shut that duck up and pull your finger free. Neither one worked, by the way."

"Derron?" Madison said through the door. "I'm

going to open the door wide enough to let the duck out. Call for help. We're going to get Miss Wanda dressed so they can come in."

"I'll need clothes," Wanda called. "Bring that pretty flowered dress. No, wait. My black pants and peach-colored blouse. The one my daughter gave me for my birthday."

"How are you going to put a blouse on?" Always practical, Sybil pointed out the obvious. "We can't get your arm in it, not with a spout attached to your finger."

"Okay, not the peach blouse," Wanda corrected, loud enough for him to hear. "Bring that ugly pink blouse with all those triangle gizmos. My daughter-in-law gave me that one."

"You hate that blouse," Sybil asked. "Why are you wearing it?"

"You'll have to cut it, right? Now I'll have an excuse not to wear it when she comes to see me." Wanda laughed again, finding her own logic hilarious.

Granny Bert was right. For a woman who was losing circulation in her hand, she was unusually chipper.

"Madison, can you get us some safety pins so we can keep the sides together once we cut it?" Sybil asked.

"There's some in the linen closet, and scissors, too." Wanda indicated the slim door with a tilt of her too-black hair. She wore it chopped off in a harsh style that did nothing for her round face and multiple chins. "Don't worry about salvaging the blouse. I say it's good riddance!"

When Derron handed the clothes through the door's narrow slit, Madison had to agree that it *was* an ugly blouse. Either the daughter-in-law had terrible taste in fashion, or she wasn't too fond of her husband's mother.

She didn't have long to ponder the thought. It was a difficult enough task getting pants onto the woman.

"He forgot my underwear! Derron, I need panties!" she bellowed, right in Madison's ear.

"Derron, there's no time for that!" Madison yelled behind her. "Seriously, Miss Wanda, we need to get you dressed before the medics get here."

"The medics?" Sybil asked sharply.

"Of course. Her entire hand is turning blue. Now help me get her pants on her. You hold them so she can put her feet in, and I'll pull them up."

While they struggled to get the rotund woman clothed, Wanda laughed as if it were all a big joke. She squealed more than once, protesting that she was ticklish. By the time they had the pants pulled up to her waist, sans underwear, all three women were exhausted.

"I hear the sirens. Let's hurry and get this blouse on you." Madison handed Sybil the scissors and the ugly blouse. "Make a slit up the side of the blouse, so we can hold it closed. I'll pin it the best I can."

Invaluable help up until now, Sybil moved in slow motion as her adrenaline leaked away. She stared at the scissors in dumbfounded fascination, unsure of what to do next. The sirens had stopped, and Madison heard Derron at the front door, urging the medics to hurry.

"Now, Miss Sybil!" Madison hissed. "Cut the left arm out of the blouse and slit it all the way up the side. Put her other arm through the right side and hand me the rest. I'll try to get her presentable."

Doing as she was told, Sybil got the blouse halfway on her friend and handed Madison the demolished left side.

"I'll pin this up the side while you button the front." Madison spoke around the opened safety pin she had clenched between her teeth. She held another in her hand, already working it through the material. She could hear rushed footsteps in the hall. "Almost done!"

she called to the paramedics.

It wouldn't win a fashion award, but the hasty closure kept most of the older woman covered as two men rushed into the room.

"Give us room to work," one of the medics said, shooing the other two women out of the confined space.

Sybil followed Madison in a bit of a daze, still clutching the scissors and the shorn sleeve in her hands. She had apparently picked both up again after buttoning the front of Wanda's blouse.

"Will she be okay?" Derron asked anxiously.

"I'm sure she will be," Madison said in a reassuring manner. She guided the younger man out of the hallway with an unsteady hand, still visualizing the disturbing shade of bluish purple that traveled up Wanda's finger and stained her hand.

They almost collided with Cutter and another fireman as the men rushed down the hall. "Which way?" Cutter asked.

"Back there. Third door," Madison provided, pointing. No one had thought to turn on the hallway light, so the space was dim with so many bodies pressed into it.

Sybil stood frozen in the hallway, still dazed by the whirlwind of events and emotions that had taken place. With her role in the emergency over and with rescuers in place, she seemed to fall apart.

"Excuse me, Miss Sybil," Cutter said. His tone was gentle but firm as he put a hand on her arm. "We need by."

"Don't push me!" she snapped.

"We need to help Miss Wanda," he insisted. "Please let us through."

Madison reached back to take her hand and tug her along. She recognized the stricken look on the older woman's face as shock. "Let's go in the kitchen," she suggested. "I'll make us some tea."

In the living room, Otis Perry stood by the door as a very agitated Lucky Ducky pecked at his feet. "Stop it, you stupid duck! Go away!" Stomping his feet only made it worse. "Go away!" he yelled as he kicked the fowl with the toe of his boot.

With a wild shriek, Sybil bolted past Madison and Derron to fling herself at the officer. "Stop that! Don't hurt that duck!" she cried, pelting him with her fists. The scissors were still in one hand, the tips biting into his flesh.

"Ouch! You stop!" he yelped, grabbing hold of her wrists.

"You're hurting Lucky Ducky!" she protested. With her hands out of commission, she resorted to using her feet.

Stunned by the behavior of the normally docile woman, it took a moment for Madison to react. "I'll get her; you get the duck!" she told Derron as they rushed forward.

Dodging her flailing feet, Otis Perry was losing his grip on her wrists. She punched him again.

"Cut it out, Sybil!" he cried.

"Miss Sybil, calm down." Madison tried grabbing the older woman by the arms, but her frail, slender body was fueled by outrage. Madison finally succeeded in yanking the scissors from her grip, but not before they drew Perry's blood.

"Sybil! Sybil, what has gotten into you!" Otis Perry seemed to be more concerned over her than he was his own wounds. "Calm down!" He finally managed to subdue her and pull her up against him, pinning her arms down by her side as his beefy arms surrounded her.

After a long moment, she batted her eyes, focused,

and was immediately appalled by a small blotch of blood oozing through his uniform. "Otis! Otis, what have I done?" she cried.

"It's okay," he assured her. "I'm fine. But are you? What happened?"

Madison was amazed at how gentle his voice sounded as he eased the woman away and assessed her trembling body. "Are you okay?"

"I-I ... yes," she said in a whispered voice. It grew stronger but no less dazed. "I saw you kicking Lucky Ducky. And-And Wanda..." She looked back over her shoulder to where emergency personnel were working on freeing her friend. "An-And I was just so upset. She's so fond of her duck, but you were hurting it. And... I don't know. I just snapped."

Madison gently pulled Miss Sybil away from the deputy and into a comforting embrace. "It's okay, Miss Sybil. It's all been upsetting, hasn't it? First Miss Wanda, then all the confusion of the medics and firemen, and then seeing Lucky Ducky being kicked. You were upset. It's okay. Let's go in the kitchen and get that tea."

"But... Otis," she said wanly. She turned to look at the deputy. "Did I hurt you, Otis? Did *I* do that to you?" Tears welled in her eyes as she saw the blood.

"It's just a scratch," he assured her. "I'm fine. You go with Madison and get that tea."

She wanted to protest. "I—"

"Go on," he urged.

His gentle tone touched Madison. There was certainly no love lost between them, but she appreciated the way he was treating the sweet older lady. If it had been Granny Bert, no doubt he would react differently. Then again, so would her grandmother. Granny Bert was tougher and stronger than her delicate best friend. The Sybil they all knew and loved was always so meek and quiet. Nothing like the hellcat that had just latched into the deputy.

Feeling generous, Madison nodded to his shoulder. "You should have the medics look at that," she said quietly.

Then she led a quietly sobbing Miss Sybil into the kitchen.

From there, she called Granny Bert.

10

Granny Bert called later that evening to give Madison a full report.

"The good news is that Wanda's going to be fine," she said. "Once they got her finger loose, the circulation returned, and she didn't need the ER. I fixed them a bite to eat and left Derron to take care of her."

"I hope you gave him strict orders to cook breakfast for Miss Wanda, not the other way around! It's ridiculous the way she pampers him."

"He was the one to bring it up. He plans to order breakfast from *New Beginnings* and bring it back to the house."

"Good for him. Now. What about Miss Sybil? How is she?"

A heavy sigh carried through the phone line. "To be honest, I'm not sure."

"I can't tell you how worried I was. How shocked. I've known Miss Sybil all my life, and I've never seen her act like that! She was absolutely livid." Madison made a small sound of distress. "It was disturbing, to say the least."

"I didn't see her like that, but I can only imagine. I've known her a lot longer than you have, and I've never even seen her out of control. I've seen her plenty mad, mind you, but she's always civil about it. She clams up and gets still, not goes off like a hellcat on attack."

"Do you think... Maybe she should see a doctor." Madison reworded what she had been about to say.

"Doctor? What makes you say that?"

She didn't want to worry her grandmother unnecessarily, but it needed to be said. "Such a drastic personality change could be a sign of a stroke," Madison pointed out gently.

"Sybil's always been so healthy." It was more denial than argument.

"Strokes can happen to anyone. Of course, it could be something else. Some sort of infection or a hormone imbalance. I really think she should see a doctor."

"I can encourage her, but for all her mild-mannered ways, Sybil has a stubborn streak a mile wide. She'll say it was nothing but worry. In fact, that's exactly what she said. She said she was worried about Wanda and seeing Otis kick Lucky Ducky was the last straw. She says her nerves couldn't take anything more, and that was the straw that broke the camel's back."

"And maybe she's right," Madison acknowledged. "Maybe it was just the stress of the moment."

"Something odd did happen, though..." Granny Bert's voice sounded perplexed.

"The whole thing was odd, so which part are you referring to?"

"Once we knew Wanda would be fine, I followed Sybil home and got her settled. I made her some spiced tea and a light snack and washed a load of laundry for her while she rested. You'll never believe who showed up right as I was leaving."

"Otis Perry."

"Yes! How did you know?"

"He looked genuinely concerned about Miss Sybil. She hit him repeatedly with the tip of the scissors, enough to draw blood. When she realized what she had done, she was visibly appalled. Surprisingly enough, he seemed more concerned by her reaction than his own injuries."

"That is surprising," Granny Bert agreed.

"It almost made him seem human."

"Let's not get carried away, now."

Madison chuckled at the comment. "Maybe that's why he came over. Maybe he wanted to assure her he was all right."

"That's what he said but to be honest, I felt strange leaving those two alone."

"You mean he stayed?" For some reason, the fact surprised her.

"Sybil more or less insisted. I reckon she needed to apologize privately, so I thought it best not to argue."

"You're probably right. The important thing is that she's calmer now."

"I think you were right about one thing, though," Granny Bert admitted. "I'll keep an eye on her. This isn't the first thing she's done that's been out of character for her."

"I did notice the new hairstyle. Now, if only Miss Wanda would get one!"

"Wanda marches to her own drum. But I'll keep an eye on Sybil and if anything else happens, I'll take her to the doctor myself."

"Sounds good. And you sound tired," Madison said frankly. "You've had a busy day taking care of two of your best friends. Maybe you should call it a night."

"I may do that. I admit, I am tuckered out."

"Okay. Good night, Granny. Love you."

"Love you, too, girl."

As she hung up, she heard Brash's voice behind her.

"I heard the *I love you* part. Tell me it was either your grandmother, Genny, or one of the kids. I'd hate to think you had a boyfriend on the sly."

Madison harrumphed. "With my grandmother, *her* best friends, and three teenagers, I don't have the energy to have a boyfriend on the sly!"

"If we're being honest here, I don't think I'd have the energy to fight off the competition."

"Sounds like your day was as bad as mine."

"We can compare notes while we're eating. I brought home something from the restaurant."

"Bless your sweet soul. After the day I've had, we may have had sandwiches or cereal."

"Hey, I do my fair share of cooking around here."

"You mean *Genny* does your share of cooking around here," she quipped.

Brash looked wounded. "Did I not bring you breakfast in bed last Saturday? Or grill steaks last week?"

"You're right. You do cook, and I do appreciate it." She reached up to drop a kiss on his lips. "What are we having tonight?"

"No clue," he said with a grin. "I called the restaurant and told them to fix me something. Genny was still there, so you know she stirred up something special."

"She really does spoil us," Madison agreed. "I'll grab the plates and the drinks, while you see what she sent."

Five minutes later, they were seated at the table, enjoying bourbon-glazed salmon on a bed of risotto, specially charred brussels sprouts, fresh greens with Gorgonzola cheese, candied pecans, and sliced strawberries, and a selection of petite desserts.

"Yep, she definitely spoils us," Brash said, scooping up another forkful of risotto. "I may be ready to face the demons of our day. You go first."

"Speaking of Genny... On the upside, I saw her husband today. Briefly. The downside is where I saw him." She paused to reinforce herself with another bite of food. "I was at Miss Wanda's, and we had to call Cutter and the fire department to the rescue."

"Her house was on fire?" He sounded more surprised than alarmed. "I didn't hear a call come in about a fire."

"No fire. More like a flood. Or it could have been if I hadn't thought to turn off the water valve."

She went on to tell him about Wanda Shanks' latest fiasco. There were times in the conversation when he had a hard time keeping a straight face.

"I would laugh, but it doesn't sound like it ended up being funny," Brash said.

"Not really. I'm concerned about Miss Sybil. It was so out of character for her, attacking Otis Perry like that!"

Her husband frowned. "I wonder why Otis didn't say anything about being injured. True, we're not on friendly speaking terms at the moment, but he's required to fill out a report on any injury, minor or otherwise, sustained while on duty."

"Why aren't you on speaking terms?"

"We speak, but it's forced. Chief to deputy. Nothing extra."

"And why is that?"

"Otis ignored a direct order. I gave explicit directions to everyone on the force that no one will go on a call alone. No exceptions, not even on a solid hunch. Otis seems to think the rule doesn't apply to him, so last night, he went out without back-up."

"Was that who called last night? I heard your phone while I was soaking in the tub. I didn't hear your words, but I heard your tone. I didn't say anything about it when I came to bed because I didn't want to upset you.

I knew how tired you were."

"It took me a while to go back to sleep. Granted, it wasn't a call, but it could have resulted in him being ambushed. He went out alone, following up on a hunch. Because he disobeyed a direct order, I took him off the duty roster and assigned him to riding with the fire department for the next two days. He's not happy about it, to say the least."

"He should have followed orders," Madison agreed.

"Even Abraham thinks I'm being harsh, but I gave the order in an effort to save their hides. We never know what we're walking into when we answer a call, but this time, the stakes are even higher."

Madison knew she had nothing to worry about where Misty Abraham was concerned. Long before Madison came back to town, Brash and the blond bombshell had casually dated. Misty was with a different department at the time, and their conflicting schedules, plus, according to Brash, their lack of commitment, made the relationship too hard to sustain. They parted on good terms, so when she later applied as a deputy with The Sisters, Brash had recommended her for the job. He and Maddy were already married, so he saw no problem with the city's decision to hire her. His new bride had a slightly different opinion but soon got over it.

For the most part, she could ignore Misty Abraham almost as well as she could ignore Otis Perry. Still, there were times like now—knowing that Brash confided in Misty and valued her opinion—that a small tendril of jealousy wound its way around her heart. It wasn't her husband's moral standards that worried her; it was the bombshell's. She knew the woman still had feelings for Brash, even if they weren't reciprocated.

Hoping to keep her voice neutral, Madison asked,

"What did you tell her?"

"That an order is an order, no exceptions. She agreed it was stupid on his part, but she thought he had a valid point about his presumed 'lead.'"

"And?"

"She thought we should at least check it out. I told her the sheriff put out a BOLO to all departments. If we see the men or the car Otis thought looked suspicious, we'll check it out. If not, we have enough on our hands without looking for more."

His words gave her hope. "So, you *do* have someone who looks suspicious?"

"That part's debatable," he said, twisting his mouth. "About half the guys around here wear tucked-in shirts, cowboy hats, and boots. The other half wear long hair, torn jeans, and baggy t-shirts. Otis described the latter half, claiming they looked suspicious. Again, that's half the population of the young men in this county."

"But he saw a car? Can't you trace the license plate number?"

"If it was a good one, yeah. But it wasn't."

"Which in itself looks suspicious, but there's no way of knowing if *they* know that," Madison reasoned. "The men could have borrowed it or bought it outright without a title. They may not realize the plates are wrong."

With exaggerated hand motions, Brash pretended to bow to her wisdom. "Exactly. Something that Abraham had trouble understanding. And probably Otis, too, for that matter. That's why we can't make assumptions at this point. We have to be open to all possibilities."

Madison blew out a sigh. "It sounds like we both had a rough day."

She didn't tell him about Delphine Craddock. If she wanted to earn the woman's trust, Madison had to use discretion when revealing private aspects of her life. Even if Brash was her husband, Delphine was her client. Maddy prided herself on confidentiality.

"It certainly sounds that way," Brash agreed.

He, too, kept some of the details of his day from her. He made a point not to discuss ongoing cases with his wife, no matter how close they were. And while there was no case against Lauri Beaver, her strange behavior would only cause Maddy to worry. The incident still baffled Brash. Something about the entire thing left him feeling off-balanced. He was more wary than worried, but the last thing he wanted was for Maddy to pick up on his unease. It was best to say nothing at all and let the incident lie.

11

The next morning, Brash called Deputy Perry into his office.

"Have a seat, Otis," he said, indicating a chair. When the older man was settled, he continued, "I understand there was an incident yesterday, and you were injured."

"Not injured," Otis was quick to say. "It was a minor scratch."

"That drew blood."

He merely shrugged. "The older I get, the easier I bleed. It was nothing."

"It was still an injury, no matter how minor, and you didn't report it."

"Because it was a scratch!"

"You received it from a woman hitting you with a pair of scissors. You know that's something you're required to report."

"It was Sybil, and it was all a misunderstanding. You know she'd never harm a fly."

"And yet you were bleeding."

"Not because she was trying to hurt me!" He sounded exasperated. "She forgot she was holding the scissors, and she was only trying to protect the duck. A duck that was determined to attack me, I might add. I think it did more damage than Sybil!" He rubbed his shin.

"Look, Otis," Brash said, leaning across his desk with a weary sigh. "You're a good officer. You're an asset to our town, and to our community."

The other man bristled. "I hear a 'but' coming."

"But you're acting like a reckless newbie, not a seasoned officer who knows the correct protocol and what's expected of him."

Otis's face turned red. "Are you firing me?"

Brash sat back in his chair, astounded. "Of course not, Otis! Where did you get an idea like that?"

"You don't seem to be happy with anything I do lately," the man sulked.

"I'm not happy with you disobeying a direct order. I'm not happy with you ignoring protocol."

"You're punishing me! You're making me ride with the FD, instead of on the streets, fighting crime."

At that, Brash had to smile. "In the two days you've been riding with the fire department, they've gone on five calls. We've gone on two. You're seeing more action with them than you would be on your normal shift with the police department."

"But—But…" Without a good rebuttal, the protest died on his lips. Otis Perry shifted in his seat. "I'm a senior officer with this department. It's degrading to be pulled from my shift."

Brash blew out a weary sigh. "Otis, it's not a demotion. It's an important role. Yes, I did it in part to make a point, both to you and the rest of the team. A direct order is just that, a direct order. Blatantly ignoring those rules comes with consequences. But there's another angle to this you're overlooking." His manner turned grave. "Otis, a member of the fire department was killed. Thank God, it's the only fatal attack any of our departments has seen, but this thing's not over yet. Yes, some of the licensed to carry volunteers are now carrying guns on their calls, but the primary focus of the fire department is to fight fires. Work wrecks. Prevent more damage to lives and property. They don't have the time or the personnel to be watching over their shoulders, waiting to be ambushed. That's why an officer is now riding with them. It's a heavy responsibility, and if I didn't feel you were capable, I wouldn't assign you to the task."

His deputy had the grace to look ashamed. "I guess I never looked at it like that," he mumbled.

"I'm not firing you, Otis. I need you. I need your help keeping our community safe, but that starts with keeping yourself safe. No solo calls, no chasing down a lead without proper backup. You understand that, right?"

"I do. And I'll abide by the rules from here on out."

"Good. You can start by filing a report on yesterday's injury."

He would have protested, but his boss' glare silenced him. It was a direct order, and he was honor bound to obey. "Yes, sir," he said quietly.

"Now that that's out of the way, I want to hear your version of the two young men you saw the day before yesterday."

Otis's round face visibly brightened. He gave an animated account of the men's appearance, their actions, and why they struck him as suspicious.

"I haven't seen anyone matching that description," Brash said when he was finished. "The sheriff put out a BOLO to all departments in the county, and to my knowledge, no one has seen the car. Your concerns have been noted and are being taken seriously."

"Something about them just seemed off, you know?"

"Yes, I do know. It's called instinct, and sometimes that's all we have to go by. At the same time, we can't let it cloud our judgment and keep us from exploring all possibilities."

"Agreed."

"Vina has already made the schedule for the rest of the week. For the next two nights, you'll be on call with the fire department. On Sunday, you'll resume your regular rotation with the police department. Barring there are no calls at night, that should give you two days to rest and to clear you head."

"My head is clear, boss."

"Good. Keep an eye on your wound so that it doesn't get infected and file that report with Vina." Brash tipped his head toward the door. "That's all."

When the call came in at midnight, Brash groaned, certain he had jinxed them with the 'no calls' thing.

When the second call came in fifteen minutes later, he was more convinced than ever.

With Otis riding along to a small grass fire just out of Naomi, Brash took the call for a possible structure fire on Sycamore Street in Juliet. There was a very real chance this was a divide and conquer strategy, but he didn't express his concerns to Maddy. No doubt she would figure that out for herself.

He did, however, express his thoughts to Cutter and Denny Goodwin as he crawled into the cab of the fire engine.

"If this is a divide and conquer trick, that will confirm more than one perpetrator. Which makes this whole situation all the more dangerous."

"We both have pistols with us, but we'll have to leave them in the truck," Cutter said. "We can't risk bullets going off in the fire. Knowing they could come from outside the perimeter is bad enough." When Brash only grunted in agreement, Cutter continued,

"Sims is riding on the tanker. Unless the fire is out of control and needs all hands on deck, he's going to be a lookout. He has a rifle with him just in case you need backup."

"Sounds like a solid plan," Brash said in approval. "I hope we're walking into a normal call, but the timing feels off. I know it's common to get two calls at once, but considering resent events, it feels suspicious."

"Even Genny picked up on that," Cutter said with a clenched jaw.

Denny nodded. "So did my wife."

"I left before Maddy could say the same thing, but I know she's thinking it."

"I wonder if our wives thought of what they were signing up for when they married us," Cutter muttered. "It can't be easy, waiting at home for us to come back. Not knowing if we'll be hurt. Or worse."

"I don't know about you," Denny said, "but I face those same worries every time I put on my bunker gear."

"We all do," Brash said. "My badge is a piece of medal. Yours is your bunker gear. We can't let fear stop us, though. Not if we're going to do our jobs."

With lights and sirens careening into the sleeping neighborhood, the engine truck pulled up to 421 Sycamore.

"I don't see any flames," Cutter noted.

"Or smoke," his partner agreed.

Scanning the area lit only by a security light, Brash acknowledged, "Could be a setup. Maybe I should check it out before you do."

"The caller said she was a neighbor a couple of streets over," Denny provided. "She wasn't sure if the owners were home, or if anyone even lived in the house."

"There's no car in the driveway," Cutter noted,

checking that his pistol was loaded. He spoke into his radio. "Sisters Fire 331, what's your ETA on the structure fire?"

"Three minutes away, tops," came the reply.

"10-4." Cutter looked over at Brash. "I'm coming with you, but let's wait for Sims. If there's a fire, I'll bring my gun back to the truck. Denny, you keep an eye out from here. If you see anyone out there, or signs of an actual fire, radio me."

The tanker truck pulled in next to them. Cutter informed them of the plan through the talk-around channel only the fire department could hear. Denny would keep watch from the hood of the truck, while Brash and Cutter circled the dark house.

With their plan decided, Brash looked over at his friend.

"Let's do this."

Across town, in a field smoldering with more smoke than flame, the brush truck arrived on scene. Otis Perry and two firemen were right behind them, riding in the other brush truck.

"If we can, drive around the edges of the fire," Otis instructed. "I'll look for signs that someone is out there, ready to ambush us." It was the primary reason for bringing the smaller truck.

"I'm not sure if we can make it all the way around, but I'll do what I can," the driver said. His partner advised the brush truck to stand down until they had the go-ahead.

"Help me look," Perry told the men with him. "Look for dark shadows. The glint of a gun. Anything that looks suspicious."

"It's hard to see in the dark," one of the men said. "And the smoke is getting thicker. We need to make this quick. This field could combust at any moment."

"You can't rush safety," Otis snapped.

"If the fire gets out, it's a safety risk of a whole different kind. In a dry field like this, we could be surrounded by flames before we pull the first hose. Not to mention how easily it could spread. There's a house two hundred yards from here. We need to get ahead of potential destruction."

"We both have our jobs to do. Mine is to save your neck," the deputy reminded him.

On the back side of the field, the truck hit a wallowed-out dip—probably from two bulls posturing their masculinity—that sent its occupants askew. The chassis rocked back and forth over the rough terrain, struggling for progress. The driver put the truck into four-wheel drive and tried pulling out of the low place, but an unseen hole was their undoing. The front disappeared from sight and lodged firmly in the hole. The first dip had left them jostled; this hole uprooted them from their seats and flung them against the dash.

Despite his bulk, Otis came out of his seat completely and banged his head against the roof. He thought he was seeing stars, until the horrifying reality sank in.

He watched as a flaming arrow arched through the air, landed in a spectacular manner, and set the field ablaze.

The field between them and the brush truck.

"We'll stick together." Brash spoke to his friend in a low voice. "We'll make a sweep around the house. I'll look for intruders; you look for flames."

Cutter disagreed. "I'll look for both. In the dark, a flame is much easier to spot. Your task is harder."

Using his high-powered spotlight, Brash swept the

light across the house and the unkept yard surrounding it. There was an empty lot on either side of the house, both of which were littered with overgrown grass and debris.

"There's a wooden fence at the back of the yard," he whispered. "An old shed of some sort on the lot to the left. Both make good places to hide."

"Noted."

They neared the back of the house. Their footsteps were light, their movements stealthy, and their voices low. "Any sign of fire?"

"None." Cutter's voice sounded grim.

"Did the caller report flames, or just smoke?"

"She just said a house was on fire. When dispatch called back, she didn't answer."

"Hmm."

Both men were thinking along the same lines.

Best-case scenario, the caller went to see if she could help or perhaps just to watch.

Worst-case scenario, it was another setup.

Either way, there were no signs of fire.

They circled the rest of the house, finding nothing. "Tell your guys they can come in," Brash said. "Approach the house with care. It's possible there's a small fire inside we can't see. It's possible this is a hoax. It's also possible it's a setup, so urge them to be on high alert."

Cutter jogged back to the fire engine, giving orders through his radio. As four of the firefighters moved in, he took the time to safely stow his weapon in the truck.

Just as he turned toward the house, Cutter saw a blinding flash of light. The windows burst from the house, sending shards of glass and wood flying into the night. His men hollered in surprise and dove for safety.

After the initial explosion, the fire died down, burning only in one specific location.

"Is everyone all right?" Cutter screamed, his ears still ringing from the blast. Glass crunched beneath his feet as he ran to check on his men. All huddled under or behind any available source of protection, no matter how small. For one, it was a scraggly bush in the front yard. For another, it was his own arms cradling his head.

"I'm fine," Denny said in a dazed voice.

"Just a little piece of glass in my arm," another said.

"Deaf, but good," the third replied. He stuck his fingers into his ears and wiggled.

"Charlie? What about you?" Cutter asked the man closest to the blast.

"Huh?" The firefighter looked at him with a blank expression.

"Are you okay?"

"What did you say?" the man yelled back.

Brash ran from around the house, yelling into his radio for help.

"Two ambulances are on the way," he told Cutter, who knelt beside the dazed fireman, talking to him in a calm, comforting voice.

"I'll take it from here," Brash assured him. He clapped Cutter on the shoulder. "Are you okay, brother?"

"My ears are ringing," the younger man admitted, "but I'm fine. If you'll get Charlie to safety, Sims and I will check out the fire."

"Be careful." Brash's voice was low and filled with concern. Who knew if a booby trap awaited them inside?

Charlie managed to get to his feet and shakily walk to the tanker.

By now, neighbors appeared from houses along the street, a siren's wail grew louder upon approach, and the police radio squawked with voices walking over one another.

"Chief! Chief deCordova, can you hear me?" a panicked dispatcher from the sheriff's office cried.

"10-4, SO, I hear you."

"Can you describe the scene? I have one ambulance almost there and another with an ETA of ten minutes. Do you need more? Do you need a bird?"

"No bird at this time. We have at least one wound with glass shards, appears superficial. One firefighter dazed and disoriented, possible concussion. Fire seems to be contained at the moment. Hold off on a third ambulance or calling other departments."

"Chief!" Before the sheriff's office could sign off, Misty Abraham's voice broke in. "Are you okay?"

"No one appears to be in immediate danger at this time, but I need you to cordon off the area."

"We're on our —"

Another frantic voice overrode Misty's transmission. "Sisters Fire to SO! Call all available departments! This grass fire on Sawyer Road is growing. We have one officer and two firefighters trapped. I repeat. Three men trapped! Send help!"

Dispatch toned out three more fire departments and two ambulance services from nearby towns.

Amid responses from each request, the sheriff's department toned out yet another call. "SO to Cougar Springs PD, we have reports of shots fired toward a residence on County Road 597. The residence belongs to a River County deputy. No word of return fire or if anyone is inside the house. Repeat. Shots fired toward a residence. Proceed with caution."

Another voice mixed into the fray. "Riverton PD to SO. We have a possible hostage situation. A security alarm was triggered at *R-Care Clinic*. The security guard isn't responding to calls. A text from his phone suggests he's a possible hostage."

Brash ran an unsteady hand up the back of his head, suppressing a cry of horror. *What the hell was happening? Had the entire county gone mad, all at one time?*

He took out his phone and shot off a quick text to Madison.

All hell is breaking loose, but I'm okay. Tell Genny that Cutter is, too. I love you. Always and forever.

12

It was a long, terrifying, horrific night. As morning broke, so did the news.

The house fire was quickly extinguished. Medics sutured cuts made by flying glass on two men; a second firefighter discovered his own wounds after the initial adrenaline rush. Charlie was transported to the hospital, where he was undergoing tests. The others, including Cutter and Brash, were treated at the scene and released, their biggest complaint being ringing in the ears.

Cutter and the remaining three firefighters responded to the grass fire on Sawyer Road. With the help of other departments, they were able to rescue the trapped men and save nearby homes. As the winds shifted, the fire spread to the tree line and continued to burn. Cutter called in the forestry department, knowing the state agency had equipment and resources their small departments didn't have.

The shots fired toward the deputy's house missed their mark. By the time units responded, the culprit was long gone.

The security guard at the clinic had been ambushed, injected with unidentified drugs, and left lying on the floor. He had been air-flighted to Houston and was listed in serious condition.

Rumors, speculation, and gossip circulated throughout the county in record speed. Phone lines hummed, friends gathered, families worried.

Law officials and all service departments met for in-depth meetings. The Texas Rangers offered their services. Agencies and departments from around the state volunteered their services. The US Marshals Service showed up unexpectedly.

The next two days were a blur for Brash, spent in one meeting after another, on one call after another, one sleepless night after another. On the third day, he finally crashed.

"Poor Daddy," Megan said, her pretty face scrunched into a worried frown. "He's going to make himself sick if he keeps this schedule up."

The teen had insisted on coming home as soon as she heard about the outbreak of attacks. She was staying at the Big House and commuting back and forth to classes. Even if she rarely saw her father, she wanted to be there for Mama Maddy.

Madison hugged the young woman close. "I know, sweetheart. I worry about the same thing. But you know your father's not one to sit still. He can't *not* be in the thick of things, trying to stop whoever's doing this."

"Sometimes, he's too noble for his own good." Tears misted her eyes.

"I know, sweetie. I know. But like I told your sister and brother, the last thing he needs right now is to be worrying about us, worrying about him. We all need to be strong and keep up as normal a facade as possible."

Bethani had spent the weekend at home, as well, and she and her brother both came during the week. Blake threatened to opt out of the baseball team. He insisted Daddy D was more important to him than any sport or any scholarship. Bethani echoed his sentiments about her own scholarship. Madison convinced them both to reconsider, insisting it was the last thing Brash wanted. Worrying about them would only distract him, something none of them could afford. She reiterated that now to Megan.

"Let's make him his favorite meal," the auburn-haired girl suggested. "He may sleep all day, straight through to morning, but at least it will be here when he's ready to eat."

"I think that's a great idea. I think I have everything we need for King Ranch Chicken."

"Grams said something about making his favorite cake and dropping it by."

"I'd invite your grandparents for dinner, but who knows if your father will even be home?"

"We could still get together, even if Daddy can't join us," Megan said wistfully. "I know we all love and worry about him. Even if he can't be here, we can support one another and keep each other company. Would it be okay if I asked them for dinner tomorrow night?"

"Of course, Meg. I think that's exactly what we all need. To form a united front and to be here to offer each other, and your father, all the support we can."

"What if we invited Granny Bert, and Cutter and Aunt Genny? I'm having withdrawals from seeing the babies, and I know this is as hard on Aunt Genny as it is you."

Smiling at her stepdaughter's thoughtfulness, Madison brushed her hand over the younger woman's vibrant auburn hair. Like she and Genny, they weren't related by blood, but they were family, nonetheless. Genny had been her best friend since the eighth grade, and all three of her children, including Megan, considered Genny their aunt.

"I don't see why we couldn't. I'll run it by your dad

before I call everyone, but I think it might take his mind off things, at least for an hour or two. I know Cutter could use the break, too."

"If he says yes, I'll see if Bethani and Blake can make it, too."

With a teasing light in her hazel eyes, Madison said, "I'm sure you'd like to invite Nate, too, but I'm not sure he and your dad can be off at the same time."

Megan wrinkled her nose. "I do like Nate," she admitted, "but right now, Daddy is my main concern. Of course, if they'd like to both be here and consider it a meeting." Behind her green-rimmed glasses, her eyes twinkled. She had multiple pairs of eye wear, to match whatever outfit she was wearing or whatever mood she was in. Today, she was dressed in green.

"Come on," Madison said, slipping an arm through hers. "Let's go see if we have everything for the casserole."

Brash was scheduled off the next evening, so their plans for an impromptu dinner came together without a hitch.

It was just the antidote to stress they all needed.

Lydia and Andrew deCordova needed the time with their son almost as much as his children and wife did. Cutter's fire-radio had been blessedly quiet all evening, and Genny needed emotional support the same as Maddy. Toddlers Hope and Faith, along with the ever-entertaining Granny Bert, added just the right amount of levity the evening called for. And Maddy was delighted to have all her children under one roof again, if only for the night. Brash often called her an old mother hen, fussing over her brood.

When Granny Bert had the chance, she got Madison off to herself. "Heard anything else from our would-be wild woman?" she asked.

Madison shook her head. "Nothing. Maybe we eased her mind enough that she's no longer worried she'll harm someone."

"If only I could convince Sybil of the same thing."

"Is she still having trouble forgiving herself for hurting Berry Perry?" It was an old nickname for the man, born from a high-school prank against the officer no one liked.

"She's better, but I know it still bothers her."

"I'm sure it does. Miss Sybil is one of the sweetest people I know. Seeing her go off the rails like that was rather shocking."

Her grandmother couldn't help but chuckle. "I wish I could have been there to see it! Otis Perry needs to be taken down a peg or two, and who better to do it than a tiny, meek little woman like my best friend?"

Giggling, they rejoined the others, where talk had turned to the dynamics of college life.

After swapping tales of parties they had attended, Madison reprimanded them. "Remember I'm still your mother, no matter how old you think you are. Be thoughtful of my ears, please."

Genny clamped her hand over her mouth in laughter. "Remember when we made that same mistake?" she asked Madison. "We were carrying on about some party we went to, telling far more than we should have ever admitted to, and Granny Bert just sat there, never saying a word."

"But the next morning, when we went to get in the car to leave, my keys were missing," Madison recalled.

Granny Bert scowled. "I told you girls back then. *I* didn't take the keys. That was your Grandpa Joe."

The Bakers had been older when they had their first and only child. Adjusting their lives to make room for Genny had been difficult. Because of their many clashes, Genny spent more time at the Cessna household than she did her own. Maddy's grandparents had become like her own. And because Maddy's parents had never truly grown up themselves, Bertha and Joe Cessna had been more like parents to her than grandparents. Titles, technicalities, and bloodlines didn't matter. They were all family.

"Stop blaming Grandpa Joe and admit you did it!" Genny laughed.

"But I didn't," the older woman insisted. "If I had thought of it, I would have done just that, but Joe was always fast on his feet. He wanted to teach you girls a lesson, while saving you from your own foolishness."

"Are you telling us that our mother—pure, sweet, innocent Madison, here—wasn't as innocent as she always claims to have been?" Blue eyes dancing, Blake gave his mother a look that made her squirm.

"Innocent? Innocent!" Granny Bert scoffed. "You're old enough now to know the truth. Your momma had a defiant streak, and sometimes it got her into a heap of trouble!"

Maddy put her hands to her suddenly hot cheeks. "Granny, my children and my in-laws are sitting at the table. You don't have to tell everything you know!"

"We don't have enough time for all that, girl." She crooked a gnarled finger at the three young adults. "I'm just saying to use the brains God gave you, do what you know is right, don't act a fool, and don't believe your momma and your Aunt Genny were saints, because I'm here to tell you they weren't."

Everyone laughed, and Madison quickly changed the subject. She wound up telling the teens about Miss Wanda's latest hijinks.

"I sure do miss her," Blake said wistfully.

"Me, too," Bethani agreed. "And Miss Sybil. They feel like they're great-aunts, or something."

"I hear both Wanda and Sybil had a stressful day.

Are they both feeling better?" the senior Mrs. deCordova asked.

Brash often accused his mother of being the Granny Bert of her generation. Not much slipped past Lydia deCordova, including events of the day in question.

"Wanda's as fit as a fiddle," Granny Bert assured her. "Not much fazes that woman. Sybil isn't doing quite as well, but I think she's coming around."

"I hear she was unusually upset."

"I picked up the aftermath, but Madison was there when it happened. She can tell you more about it than I can."

All eyes turned to her granddaughter. "It was rather surreal," she said. "The entire *thing* was surreal. Did you know that Miss Wanda bathes Lucky Ducky in her bathroom sink? Sans clothes?"

Bethani looked horrified. "Please tell me you're referring to Lucky Ducky."

"Him, too."

Blake flung his arm over his eyes. "Ugh! That is not a sight I want burned into my corneas!"

"Imagine my poor eyes," his mother said. "I had to help her get dressed before the medics and the fire department got there."

Andrew hadn't heard the story before, so he asked his daughter-in-law, "Why did you have to help her? And why were emergency crews there?"

"This is Wanda Shanks we're talking about," Madison reminded him. "When her sink faucet wouldn't shut off, she put her finger in it to plug it up, and then her finger got stuck. Miss Sybil happened to stop by, tried to help, and couldn't. She called Derron, Derron called me, and I didn't have much more success, other than to get the valve shut off and clothes on Miss Wanda before the medics arrived."

"Oh, you poor dear," Lydia murmured.

"Thankfully, all the pertinent parts were covered when I arrived," Cutter said. "But I did notice how strange Miss Sybil was acting."

"I think once the adrenalin high petered out," Madison speculated, "she just fell apart. Then she saw Perry kicking her friend's pet duck, and she just sort of... lost it. She flew into him like a wet hen."

"I wish I could have seen that!" Genny grinned. She and Deputy Perry went way back, and their past was even more contentious than his and Madison's.

Granny Bert had to agree. "Of course, now Sybil feels all kinds of guilt. She can't believe she acted that way."

"Maybe she should treat herself to another session at that new spa in town," Lydia suggested. "I understand she and Wanda go there quite often."

"Where is that?" Bethani asked. "I didn't know there was a spa in town. Do they do pedicures?"

"I think so, but I've not been in yet, myself," Lydia said. "Bertha, do you know?"

"I don't go in for that nonsense," Granny Bert sniffed.

"You don't like pedicures?" Megan asked in surprise.

"I never did care much for someone else touching my feet, but that's not the nonsense I meant. I meant all those oils and lotions she uses."

"That who uses? I guess there's been more happening in town than I realized." Bethani frowned, and Megan echoed the expression.

"Miss Zuri. She's some Creole woman who opened up a spa a few doors down from *The Gift Co-Op*. *Miss Zuri's Essentials*, she calls it. Sells all sorts of snake oil, only she calls them *essential* oils," Granny Bert harrumphed. "She mixes up teas, spices, and lotions, and burns incense, too. I wouldn't put it past her to mix up potions, either."

"Potions?" Madison asked. She hadn't made it into the new business, either.

"Something like that," her grandmother insisted. "I swear, that's why Wanda's so happy these days. I think she's getting some sort of happy potion from that woman."

"I thought Miss Wanda was always happy," Blake said. "That's what makes her so much fun."

"Her new version of happy is over-the-top happy," Granny Bert groused.

Madison twisted her mouth in thought. "She did seem to laugh a lot for someone whose finger was turning blue because it was stuck in a faucet."

Granny Bert nodded. "Mark my words, that Madam Zuri woman is giving her some sort of silly serum. Wanda doesn't need any help in the silly department."

"I thought it was Miss Zuri, not Madam Zuri."

"Same difference." Her grandmother shrugged. "No matter what she calls herself, I say she's practicing voodoo."

"Voodoo? Like casting spells on people?" Bethani asked, her eyes wide.

Madison brushed away the idea. "There's no such thing as casting spells on people. You can play with their psyche. Manipulate them into believing something other than the truth. Play with their minds and into their weaknesses. But you can't cast spells."

"Really?" Brash teased. "Because I could swear you cast a spell on me."

His father, the perfect specimen of what Brash would look like in thirty years, grinned from the other end of the table. "It must be a weakness that runs in the family." He draped his arm across his wife's shoulder. "I say the same thing about your mother."

Granny Bert wasn't swayed by their playfulness.

"Well, if she's not casting spells, Miss Zuri must be slipping alcohol into those tea leaves and lotions of hers, because Wanda is more happy-go-lucky than ever. Just like she is when she has her margaritas or her mariju...er, her special medicine." She glanced over at her great-grandchildren, quickly changing her words.

The girls' mouths fell open. "Miss Wanda uses marijuana?" Bethani cried.

"I don't believe it!" Megan said with a giggle. Actually, it made perfect sense now that she thought about it.

"No wonder she's so much fun," Blake agreed. His dimples appeared when he grinned. "Who knew?"

13

The family dinner was a nice reprieve, but it was back to reality the next day.

Brash had stalled the press as long as possible, but after Friday night, there was no hiding the truth from the public. It was better to tell the official version rather than the embellished tales running rampant about town. Dane Cessna, owner and editor of the local newspaper, wanted a quote for a story about the recent attacks. Brash trusted Madison's cousin to do the truth justice, so he spent a half hour answering questions the best he could.

As he hung up, his attention was pulled in another direction.

"Chief?" Misty Abraham knocked on his door and poked her head inside. "We have reports of two men seen walking around town. They fit the description of the ones Otis reported. Shall I take a look?"

"Who's riding with you?"

"Uhm... you?" she asked hopefully. "Schimanski just stepped out for lunch."

"Let me get my hat," Brash said, pushing away from his desk and standing. His knee popped in protest, which he ignored. Football injures could haunt a man for life.

Five minutes later, they were cruising the streets of Juliet.

"Where were they seen?" Brash asked.

"Cedar Street. Someone else saw them over near the high school."

"I don't understand the sudden calls about these two." Brash's brow puckered. "The sheriff issued a BOLO to the departments, not to the general public. Why the sudden interest? Have they committed a crime?"

"Just the crime of being a stranger in a small town," she said with a grimace. She cast him an apologetic look. "You know it's true. One caller described the young men as derelicts."

"There's a word I haven't heard in a while," he mumbled.

"Older woman," she said by way of explanation. "Lived here for years, she said, and not used to seeing strangers walking around in raggedy jeans and shaggy hair. Her words, not mine."

"Well, I don't see them now. Let's take a drive out by the school. If they are troublemakers, that's the last place they need to be."

"I'm almost expecting to see two men with the words 'Bad Guys' tattooed across their foreheads. They must be some seriously evil-looking *derelicts,*" Brash predicted.

Before they reached The Sisters ISD, they saw two young men sitting cross-legged on the side of the road, well out of the way of traffic. The men turned to look at them, their faces free of tattoos, facial hair, and evil expressions.

"Or maybe not," Misty said as she eased off the road and drew to a stop.

"Stay here with your radio handy," Brash

murmured to her as he opened the door. He put on a friendly smile and got out of the car. "You fellas having trouble?" he called.

Both young men stood, all lanky limbs and awkward movements. They were obviously younger than they looked. Twenty, at the most, but Brash guessed younger.

"Nah," the taller of the two said. "We were just walking around town and got tired."

Brash kept his tone conversational. "No car?"

"His uncle sold us a clunker, but it only runs half the time," the boy said, hitching his thumb toward this friend.

"That's a bummer," Brash commiserated. "You fellas new in town?"

"Just visiting. I came down to help my grandma, and Jeff, here, came with me."

"I should have introduced myself. Brash deCordova."

The boys politely took his offered hand and shook.

"Landon Rossi," the taller of the two said.

"Jeff Michaels."

"Welcome to The Sisters." Until he had a legitimate reason to suspect the young men, Brash meant his words. They both seemed well-mannered and respectful. The fact that they stood and shook his hands impressed him; so often these days, the younger generation failed to grasp the rules of polite society.

"Yeah, we were wondering about that," Jeff said, cocking his head sideways. "The population signs say Juliet and Naomi, but the welcome sign coming off the highway says The Sisters. Which is it?"

A smile tweaked Brash's lips. The question was often asked. "All, actually. The towns were named after two sisters, one on either side of the railroad tracks. They share most of the same services—water, police, fire department, school—so most people just call it 'The Sisters.' It confuses a lot of people."

"I know why," Jeff mumbled.

Brash's tone remained smooth as he transitioned to investigator mode. "That car your uncle sold you. Does it happen to be an older model Ford Grenada?"

"Yeah, like ancient. Baby blue," Jeff said in distaste. "It was my aunt's. Sissy color, but the only thing we could afford."

Landon looked at the officer warily. "Uhm, why do you ask? Did we run a stop sign or something?"

"Not that I know of. I was just asking. Several people have noticed it around the county. Parked alongside the road, at a gas station in the Indian Meadows community..." Brash named the places causally, but his eyes keenly watched for their reaction.

Landon rolled his eyes. "That crap car broke down on us more times than just that," he complained. "No wonder it only cost us three hundred bucks."

His disgust seemed genuine, but Brash knew that some people were better actors than others. "Did you fellas hear what happened at the gas station later that night?"

"Dude, that was tragic!" Jeff said. His eyes were wide.

Landon nodded in agreement. "The man who owned the station said it was okay to leave the car there overnight. We came back later and got it started. It took us a while, but we rolled out about midnight. I guess we barely missed the fire." He shook his shoulder, as if to dispel the negative thought. "I heard a guy died."

"Unfortunately, yes. Did you see any smoke?" Brash asked. The boy used the word 'fire,' even though no actual flames had broken out. He didn't mention shots being fired. *Maybe*, Brash thought, *their story was legit.*

Landon shook his head, slinging blond hair out of his eyes. "Nah, it looked normal when we were there."

"Did you see anyone or anything that looked suspicious?"

Brash didn't miss the look that passed between the two.

"What?" he asked.

"It, uh, wasn't anything, really," Jeff mumbled, not meeting Brash's eyes.

"Landon? Is that what you think?" Brash's voice was sharper than before, without being accusatory. "That it was nothing?"

"Uh, yeah, I guess."

"If you men know anything, it's important that you tell me. It could help our case tremendously."

"Case?" Landon picked up on the word. "Was it arson? Is that why that firefighter died? Dude. That's really messed up."

Without answering directly, Brash repeated, "If you can tell us anything, anything at all, it will be a big help."

After an uneasy glance toward his friend, Landon's shoulders sagged. "There were these guys…" he said with obvious reluctance. "They stopped to ask if we needed help. They had that look, you know?"

"What look?"

"They looked like trouble," Jeff supplied.

"What were they driving?"

"Two of them rode motorcycles, two others were in a souped-up Camaro."

"What color was it?"

Landon answered, "Dark, but I couldn't tell the exact color. The light wasn't the best out there, which was part of the reason it took us so long to get the car fixed." He looked at his friend. "I say it was dark blue. You?"

Jeff shrugged. "Could have been black." He looked at Brash. "But it had those big rims, you know?"

"Can you describe the men?" Brash flipped open the small notebook he kept tucked into his front pocket, already jotting down notes.

"One was a white dude, for sure. Two looked Latino, or maybe half. One of them was darker than the other, so he could have been half black. The fourth guy was definitely black. They all wore chains and had tattoos. Not like mine." He indicated his own arms. One had dragons, lizards, and swords that would eventually become part of a full arm-sleeve. In contrast, his other arm had a single rose, with a girl's name written beneath it. "Theirs," he continued, "were like... everywhere. Even on their necks."

"Theirs were graphic, too. Not like ours." Jeff indicated an arm similar to his friend's. "It was dark, but I could see enough to know these were dudes we didn't want to mess with."

"What else did they say?" Brash asked. It was a possible break in the case, and he needed all the details he could gather.

"Uhm, they offered us some weed," Jeff volunteered, glancing at his friend.

"Anything harder?"

"Yeah," Landon admitted. "At least one of them was high. The others looked more like pushers than users."

"What else?" He sensed there was more.

Another glance between them, another uneasy detail. "They didn't say it in so many words," Landon said, "but, uh, they're part of a gang. They were feeling us out, seeing if we wanted in."

"And what did you say?"

The young man gave a harsh snort of humorless laughter. "We're smart enough not to flat-out refuse, but we didn't show interest, either. We don't mess with guys like that. They said they'd see us around, and they drove off."

"Which way did they go?"

"Left out of the parking lot," Jeff said. "Not sure which way that is."

"Toward Riverton."

"Is that where the Dairy Queen is?"

Brash bit back a smile. He recognized that look in Jeff's eyes. Blake was a big fan of the place, too. "Yes," he said. "It's the county seat."

"Not sure why they'd want to go where there's more cops, but whatever. I think they're from a big town, anyway," he said.

"Did they say which one?"

"No. But they made cracks about all the one-horse towns around here. Said something about easy pickings." He glanced over at his taller friend.

Brash's eyes narrowed. "As in thefts? Buyers?"

"Maybe," Landon answered the question. "We thought... maybe gang members."

"Or as in a good place for gang initiations?" Brash's blood chilled at the thought.

"That, uh, was sort of the impression we got."

"We hope we never see those dudes again," Jeff agreed. "We don't want trouble."

"Well, walking everywhere makes you easy targets," Brash pointed out. "Can I offer you a ride?"

"You're arresting us?" Landon asked, clearly panicked.

"No, nothing like that. Just offering you fellas a ride. Who did you say your grandmother was? Tell me where she lives, and I'll drop you off."

"She's new in town. Lives over on North River Oaks in Naomi."

"Come on, then. You've been a lot of help, and I'd like to repay the favor. It will save you a long walk."

"Look, dude," Landon started. He stood straighter and corrected himself. "Sir. We appreciate the offer, but we gotta think about how it would look if these guys saw us with cops. If they saw you take us home, and not to the station, they might think we ratted them out. Which we sort of did, but they can't ever know that. You'll keep it on the downlow, right?"

"Of course. I would never jeopardize the safety of a witness."

Jeff paled. "W-We're witnesses? To what?"

"Poor choice of words on my part," Brash was quick to say. "But I give you my word. I'll keep you out of it if I ever come across these men." He pulled two cards from his pocket and handed them to each young man. "This is my personal cell number. If you see them again or think of anything else, please call me."

"This sounds serious," Landon said, staring down at the card in his hands.

"It is." Brash tucked his notebook away. "You've been a big help, and I appreciate your cooperation. I understand why you don't want a ride, so this is for anyone who might be watching." He took a few steps toward the car, turned back around with a convincingly stern look on his face, shook his finger at them, and spoke loudly, "You two better stay out of trouble. You hear me? I'll be watching."

As soon as he slid back into the car seat, Misty pounced. "We're not taking them in for questioning?"

"No. These aren't the guys we're looking for."

"But you told them you'd be watching. You shook your finger at them! What was that all about?"

With a pleased smile, he asked, "So, it worked? It looked convincing?"

"Of course it looked convincing! I know that look you had on your face! What is going on, Brash? Are you saying it was all an act?"

"Yep. Those two are little more than kids, and well-mannered ones, at that. They aren't our suspects, but they did give us the best lead we've had so far."

"And you're just letting them walk away?" his deputy asked in disbelief. "Don't you need to verify what they told you?"

"Call it instinct, but I believe what they told me. And I don't like it. Not one bit."

"Could you please be a little more forthcoming and tell me what's going on?" she asked irritably. Because of their long-ago involvement, she sometimes forgot to speak to him as her superior.

"They do drive the old Grenada, which they bought from the dark-haired boy's uncle. For three hundred bucks, if that tells you anything. Their names are Landon and Jeff, they're here visiting Landon's grandmother who's new in Naomi, and the car has left them broken down more times than they care to count. Last week, it conked out on them at *Crane's Gas Station*. They went back to work on it later that night and got it running about two hours before the smoke alarm went off. From what I gathered, they think Jose Robles died from a fire, not a gunshot wound."

"They could be lying."

"I don't think so."

"Did they see anything that looked suspicious?"

"Not so much any*thing* as any*one*." He ignored her exasperated sigh. "Four rough-looking characters stopped and offered to help. They offered a whole lot more, too. Weed, hard drugs, and possible involvement with a gang."

"You can't be serious!"

"I wish. They didn't come out and say they were part of a gang, but the implication was there, according to Landon and Jeff. What's worse, they think they're in this area because it makes a good place to initiate new members."

Misty Abraham went pale. "Don't tell me... you think these attacks are gang related? Part of an initiation process!" The last was an outrageous statement, not a question.

"Like I told you before, we can't make assumptions. We have to be open to all possibilities. But, yes, gang initiations are one of the possibilities we need to consider."

"This is scary, Brash," she breathed.

"I know small towns aren't immune to crime and drugs or even organized crime. We've already seen it too often, right here in The Sisters. But gangs are a new element. And a very dangerous one, especially for our youth."

"In a twisted way, a gang makes sense. After Friday night, I think it's obvious this is the work of more than just one, or even two, people. There were four attacks, almost simultaneously. That took coordination and people." Her hands tightened on the steering wheel. "We have to stop this."

"Agreed. As soon as we get back to the station, I'll call the sheriff and report my suspicions." He stared out the side window and sighed. "I see more county-wide department meetings in my very near future. And a lot more sleepless nights."

14

Brash called home later that afternoon. "Don't bother waiting on me for dinner. I have a meeting. They're feeding us, so I have a feeling it may run late."

"New lead?" Madison asked.

"Maybe, but it's still too soon to say. Why don't you treat Megan to dinner out tonight? It will do you good. You've both been worrying too much lately, as it is."

"With good reason. But you're right. Going out sounds like a great idea."

Megan was more than receptive to the idea, so that evening, they found themselves at *Montelongo's*, munching on crispy tortilla chips and salsa while they waited on their entrees.

"Daddy has a lead?" The auburn-haired beauty adjusted the vibrant blue glasses on her nose. They matched today's pair of leggings and the long necklace swinging against her long-tailed white blouse. Megan always wore clothes that were as trendy and coordinated as Derron's, and the exact opposite of her stepmother's. Everyone teased Madison about wearing clothes from Granny Bert's closet, but she chose to think of her understated wardrobe as classic.

"He sounded cautiously optimistic, so yes, that's the

impression I got."

"I hope they catch these people soon, so we can all breathe easier, and our lives can go back to normal."

"Sweetheart, your father appreciates you being here, but you don't have to stay, you know. He understands you have a busy schedule with college."

"I'm not just here for him. I'm here for you, too, Mama Maddy." She reached out to grip her stepmother's hand. "I *need* to be here. For him, for you, and for me. So unless you're kicking me out..."

"Never!"

"Then until further notice, you're stuck with me."

After they had an enjoyable dinner and walked to the parking lot, Madison saw Delphine Craddock and two young men getting out of a nearby car.

"Hello, Delphine," Madison greeted the woman with a polite smile.

"Oh, Madison! I didn't expect to see you here." She looked surprised but pleased. The welcoming smile on her face pegged her as anything but a killer.

"We just had a wonderful dinner, but I promise, we left enough for you. This is my daughter Megan. Megan, this is Delphine Craddock. She recently moved here."

"Hello, Megan. What beautiful hair you have! Oh, and this is my grandson Landon, and his friend Jeff. They're down here getting me settled in."

Both young men looked at Megan with appreciation. It took them a moment to notice Madison had extended her hand in introduction. She smiled, most of it directed to their reaction to her stepdaughter.

"Madison deCordova," she said.

Landon politely dragged his eyes off the beautiful young woman. "Nice to meet you." As an afterthought, he asked, "Did you say deCordova?"

"Yes, that's right."

"We met a Brash deCordova this morning."

"That's my father," Megan said in obvious pride. "He's the chief of police in The Sisters."

"Yeah, he explained the whole Sisters thing to us," Jeff said. "It's a little confusing for newcomers."

"I'm sure it is," Megan agreed, her twinkling laughter enchanting both males. "I've lived here since I was a baby, so it seems normal to me."

Delphine looked sharply at her grandson. "How did you meet the chief of police? Was he questioning you?"

"Uhm, not really. Well, yes, but in a friendly way. He saw us resting on the side of the road and offered us a ride." He deliberately omitted some of the details.

"To jail, I suppose?" she asked in a cold voice.

"No, Grandma. To your house." He looked not only confused by her reaction but embarrassed. He dared a glance at Megan, who looked just as confused.

Something in Delphine's voice made Madison feel uneasy. The now scowling woman sounded much like she had the first time she called, claiming she wanted to harm someone. Madison wondered if she was having another one of her anger flashes.

"Delphine?" she asked softly, touching her elbow. "Are you okay?"

"Wh-What? Oh. Yes. Yes, I'm fine." She didn't sound convincing.

Someone called her name, and Megan whirled to see Nate Stone coming toward her. She paused for a moment, admiring how handsome he looked in his uniform, before hastily excusing herself and meeting him halfway. As their heads dipped in conversation, Madison felt Delphine stiffen beneath her light touch.

"Delphine?" she repeated.

In a taut voice, Delphine turned to her grandson. "Would you boys mind going in and getting us a table?"

They left with reluctance, eyes lingering on Megan and the man she talked to.

Noticing the way Delphine glared at the young couple, Madison wondered if she found Megan's behavior offensive. Admittedly, Delphine had just introduced her grandson to the girl, and in the next moment, she had run to meet another man. Delphine had no way of knowing the two were seeing one another, or that Megan hadn't meant her actions as a slight to her new acquaintances.

"Who is *that*?" Delphine asked the question as if it left a bitter taste in her mouth.

"Deputy Nate Stone, one of the officers here in The Sisters." Madison offered a slight frown, followed by a light chuckle. "I'm never sure of today's lingo, but in my day, we would say they were casually dating."

"She's dating a *cop*?"

"Again, dating may not be the right word these days. But they are seeing one another, yes." The glare on Delphine's face worried her. "Delphine? Is it happening again? Are you feeling angry?" Moving so that she blocked sight of Megan and Nate, Madison put slight pressure on the other woman's arm, hoping to make her feel grounded.

It seemed to have worked. Delphine batted her eyes a few times, slowly focusing her gaze on Madison's concerned face. "Y-Yes. Yes, it just hit me out of the blue! That's the way it always does. For no reason whatever, I—I feel the rage coming over me, and there's nothing I can do about it." Delphine dropped her face into her hands. "Why is this happening to me? I'm not a violent person! So why do I act like this?"

Madison wondered the same thing. "This may sound like an odd question," she said after a moment, "but... did you ever have a bad experience with a redhead?"

Delphine looked up, completely confused by the question. "What?"

"I know it sounds odd, but it was right after you met Megan, and after you mentioned her auburn hair, that you started... acting strange."

"I acted strange? You noticed it?"

"Yes, I did. So did your grandson."

She looked frightened. "Wh-What did I do?"

"The tone of your voice changed, and you looked angry."

"I did? I don't even remember that. I just know I felt angry. Angry enough to... Oh, Madison! This is so frightening! What if I hurt Landon? Or Jeff?"

"Let's not jump to conclusions. Maybe it's the color red. Maybe you associate it with something negative that happened in your past."

"Like a bull?" she asked, neither offended nor amused. She seemed contemplative. "I see red and want to charge?"

"Something on that order."

"Hmm," she considered. "Well, I was in my car that day—my *red* car— when I had the urge to slam into the car in front of me."

"What about the other times? Do you remember if you happened to see the color when the feeling came over you before?"

"Maybe?" She made it a question. "That one day I was shopping, so it's possible I saw something red. I don't remember anything specific, that day or any of the others."

"Of course, that may not be it. It was just a thought."

"Something I should consider, I suppose." She looked toward her car. "I'm looking at my car now, and I don't feel anything, but maybe I should consider buying a new one. It has quite a few miles on it already."

"Don't do anything hasty," Madison urged, "on my very uneducated speculation. I'm mostly wondering out loud."

"At this point, I'll consider anything."

Keeping her voice soft, Madison dared to ask, "Including seeing a doctor?"

Delphine nodded her gray head. "I called my doctor back home and asked him to make a recommendation. I haven't heard back yet, but when I do, I promise I'll call and make an appointment."

"Good. I think that's a very wise decision."

"Well, thank you yet again, Madison. I suppose I should get inside. The boys will be wondering what happened to me."

"Call me anytime, Delphine. I mean it. I want to help."

Driving back to the Big House, Megan ventured to say, "That woman back there. Delphine? Is she okay? I mean, like in the head?"

"I want to say yes, but the truth is, she's having some issues lately."

"Who is she? How do you know her?"

"She's a client, actually."

"Oh. She seemed nice at first, but then it seemed like something came over her, and she turned hostile. Was I the only one to notice? I think her grandson felt it, too, though. He looked embarrassed by her change in behavior."

"No, we all definitely noticed it."

"Is she on some kind of medication, I hope?"

"I know she's trying to get a doctor's appointment." It was the only comment Madison felt free to make.

"Maybe she needs to go to that new spa and get some of Miss Wanda's happy juice." As a thought occurred to her, Megan turned in her seat and said in an excited voice, "Hey! That's what we need to do! I don't have classes tomorrow afternoon, so I could come home early, and we can go to the spa. If it's okay with you, we could ask my mom to join us."

"You know I wouldn't mind at all," Madison said.

There was a time, back in high school, when Madison viewed Shannon Wynn as her arch enemy. But time and maturity—and Megan—had changed that. Madison admired Shannon for raising such a sweet, considerate, well-adjusted daughter. The two women shared a love for the girl, and, in truth, a love for Brash. Shannon no longer loved her ex-husband romantically and was happily married to Matt Aikman. With their contentious marriage behind them, she had come to love Brash as a good friend and as the father of their child.

Madison understood. She felt the same way about Gray. Their marriage had died long before his fatal car crash, but a part of her would always love him. They had been happy once upon a time, and he had given her the greatest treasure ever in their twins.

Now, with the past long behind them, Madison and Shannon had become friends and enjoyed spending time together. She had no objections to including her in a mother-daughter-stepmother outing.

"Perfect!" Megan beamed. "I'll call her right now and make sure she's free!"

While Megan called her mom, Madison saw a text from Brash. The meeting hadn't lasted as long as he feared, and he was on his way home.

Megan stayed downstairs for a while to visit, then vanished to her third-floor bedroom.

"The meeting went better than expected?" Madison asked, curling her feet under her as she sat next to Brash in the family room. When the house was remodeled, the designers called it a media room, but the term sounded too cold for her tastes. She preferred calling it something homier.

"It was shorter than expected, anyway."

"That doesn't sound too encouraging."

"Manning was being difficult, as usual."

"Can you tell me about your lead?"

He hesitated, knowing it would only cause more worry. She already worried enough as it was.

Instead of answering, he moved his fingers through her hair. "Did you know it would be like this when you married me?" he asked quietly.

She smiled. "Do you mean did I know it would be this wonderful? No. It's far better than I ever dreamed it could be."

"No, I mean this dangerous. This frightening. Did you know you would spend your days worrying, wondering if I would come home at night?"

"What brought this on?" she asked, wondering at his solemn mood.

"Everything that's been happening lately. The new worry lines I see in your face. The fear in your voice, every time my phone rings at night. All of it."

Realizing he was serious, Madison took her time answering. "I knew your job could be dangerous. Even though this is a small town, there's still crime. Still mean people in the world, and in this community." She tucked herself under his arm.

"It's not just here in River County," she continued. "It's everywhere. There's a new anti-cop sentiment in the world, and it scares me to death. Most people focus on the bad cops. The ones who are corrupt and evil, the ones who need to be behind *bars*, not behind badges. Every time a bad cop kills an unarmed suspect—or when a good cop makes a bad judgment call— the hate grows. Social media makes it even worse. Someone posts their opinion, and people mistake it for truth. No one's talking about all the good things police officers do. The way you put your lives on the line for people every single day. You're willing to die for people you don't know. People you don't like. Even the people who don't like you."

"Ironically, those are the people who accuse us of profiling, when they do the same thing to us. They assume one bad cop means all bad cops."

"Yes, and there are many who believe them. Even worse, people right here in our area have bought into that theory. They think anyone wearing a badge is the enemy, and they've waged a war against you."

"So? Back to my question. Do you regret getting yourself into this mess?"

"Never, Brash. I could never regret marrying you."

"Even when you realize how heavy this badge is that I wear? I'm not the only one bearing the weight of it. You are, too. All wives, or husbands, share the burden with us. Our kids and parents carry the weight. We signed up for this. You didn't."

"I knew you were an officer of the law when I chose to marry you. Maybe I didn't envision this new danger you're in—I don't think any of us did—but I knew there was danger. There's danger simply in living. But the life I have with you is worth it. I could never regret it." She laid a hand atop the badge still pinned to his shirt. "I will proudly bear the weight of this badge with you."

After a very long and tender kiss, they sat for a while in silence, wrapped in each other's arms. Brash spoke at last.

"I didn't say this when you first asked because I didn't want you to worry. But you do, anyway, so I may as well tell you. We do have a lead. It may or may not pan out, but it's the first ray of hope we've had in finding our suspects."

"I notice you're using the plural now."

"After this weekend, I think I have to, don't you?"

"Sadly, yes."

"It gets worse." After a moment's hesitation, he said it. "We have reason to believe this may be gang related."

Madison couldn't hide her gasp. "Here? In The Sisters?"

"River County, at any rate. It may not be, but there's a distinct possibility. And like Abraham said, in a twisted way, it sort of makes sense. They have no respect for authority unless they're the ones demanding it."

"Could this be some sort of initiation, do you think?"

"That's what I'm thinking. If, of course, that's who we're dealing with. We could be way off base. But if it is a gang, I'd rather it be an initiation than a clear case of them moving into the community."

"Why's that?"

"Sometimes with initiations, they choose locations where they're less likely to be caught. Or so they think."

"Obviously, they've never come up against the very stubborn, very determined, very astute Brash deCordova."

"I'd rather think of it as a very dedicated Brash deCordova."

"That, too." Needing to lighten the conversation, she ran her fingers along his strong jawline. "Not to mention a very handsome one."

"I hardly think my looks matter in this instance."

"They might, if it's a gang full of women."

"There's only one woman I'm interested in, and she's so busy talking, I can't even kiss her."

"I won't say another word."

15

"Ahhh. This is the life," Shannon Aikman said, her face the perfect picture of contentment. "I may have died and gone to Heaven."

"If not," Madison agreed, eyes shut in utter bliss, "this wouldn't be a bad way to go. In fact, I think it might be perfect."

They relaxed in a softly lit room at *Miss Zuri's Essentials,* taking advantage of the massage chairs before going in for individual, hands-on massages.

Megan had to agree. "I may never move again."

Even though it had been Megan's idea to come here, she didn't sound as bubbly as she normally did. Madison hoped her subdued tone was simply a sign of pure relaxation. The whole idea of today was to leave their troubles behind and take time to relax.

"What do you think was in that lotion they use?" Madison mused. "It smells divine."

"Doesn't it, though?" Shannon inhaled before answering. "Miss Zuri said it's her own creation. A special blend of essential oils and herb extracts. I asked."

"Let me guess. It's a secret formula."

"Passed down from her grandmother who was a

voodoo priestess. One of New Orleans' finest, according to her. Which explains this magical spell I'm under." Shannon all but swooned.

"I'm surprised to see how busy this place is. And from what I can tell," Madison said, "Miss Zuri does all the massages herself. I don't see how she manages it. She has to be in her seventies."

With her eyes closed, Madison couldn't see the playful glint in her stepdaughter's eyes, but she heard it in her voice. "I hear Cajun voodoo queens have some superpower that lets them live long lives."

"Unlike their enemies?" Madison teased, opening one eyelid.

"Something like that."

The tunes floating out from the speakers were soft and low, a blend of gentle humming and lyrical chants, with a hint of tribal music playing in the background. The harmonious words were indistinguishable and spoken in an unfamiliar language, but they had an undeniable message of peace and relaxation. The three women soaked up the atmosphere, embracing the calm mood.

"I am ready for you now," a lilting voice spoke from the doorway. Miss Zuri, wrapped in flowing shirts and a colorful turban atop her head, smiled at them in her mystical way. She crooked a finger at Shannon. "Come, pretty lady. You will go first."

Scampering out of her chair, Shannon waved as she followed the dark-skinned woman from the room.

"Enjoying yourself?" Madison asked her stepdaughter. "You had a good idea in coming here."

"I definitely needed it, after the day I had!" Megan huffed.

"Hard class?"

"Not exactly."

Hearing the hesitancy in her words, Madison pried

open one eyelid. "What is it, honey?" she asked in concern. Both eyes came open, and she sat up straighter in the chair. "You've acted distracted all afternoon."

"Can I tell you something?"

"Of course. You can tell me anything."

"I didn't want to say anything in front of my mom, but I had a bad experience before I picked you two up."

"I noticed you looked a little flustered. What happened?"

Megan proceeded haltingly, clearly nervous. "I stopped for gas at the *Gas 'n Go* out on the highway. I normally get it at Mr. Rudy's, but I was almost on empty—I know, foolish on my part—so I pulled in at the first station I came to. There were these... guys..." Her eyes didn't quite meet her stepmother's. "Men, really. Rough-looking men. There were four of them, and they were all wearing chains and leather jackets and spikes on their boots. They were riding motorcycles."

A cold fear invaded the aura of peace surrounding Madison. Was this the gang Brash had mentioned? "Were they bothering you?" she asked sharply.

"At first, it was just whistling and a few flirty comments. Some of the comments were more crude. I ignored them, but one of the guys was persistent. He came over on my side of the pumps and tried to take the hose from my hands. He pretended to be a gentleman, offering to fill my tank, but some of his remarks were... suggestive. So was the way he looked at me. I told him no and decided five gallons was all I needed."

"Good for you!"

"There was a problem taking cards at the pump, so I had to go inside to pay. But when I tried to pass, the men wouldn't let me. I mean, they didn't physically stop me, but they stood between me and the door. Their expressions dared me to push past them. When I tried going around them, they moved, too. They just laughed." A shudder worked through her body. "It was one of the most evil things I've ever heard."

"Why didn't you call your father?"

"I know how busy he is, trying to find who's behind these attacks. And I thought I could handle it. It was broad daylight, and there were other people around."

"Did any of them notice what was going on? Did anyone help you?"

"Thankfully," Megan nodded, relief evident in her voice, "someone did. Just when I was getting really concerned, a patrol car pulled up. Deputy Perry crawled out of the passenger's seat, and for once, I was happy to see him. He pulled up his service belt like he was all big and bad, waddled over, and asked if there was a problem. I could tell he was a little nervous, but he walked up to them like he meant business."

"What happened next?" Madison asked on bated breath.

"The men made a few remarks, like 'no one called the donut chuckers,' or 'we don't need no Nazi of the Republic round here.' One spat at his feet and said something really rude. Another one bowed up on him, but Perry didn't back down. I really didn't think he had it in him, but he kept his cool and didn't let them get to him."

"So, they just left?"

"Not at first. Then Perry said something I wish he hadn't, but he did."

"What did he say?"

"He told them they didn't know who they were messing with. He told them my dad was the chief of police, and that only fools went up against him. He said he didn't take them for fools, so they'd be better off leaving town."

"And?"

"One of them looked a little shaken up, but the other seemed to take it as a challenge. And the way they looked at me…" She shivered again. "Deputy Perry told me to get in my car, and that he would pay for my gas. One of the firefighters was riding with him, so he motioned for him to get out. While the fireman—I think his name is John? —walked me to my car, I heard Perry radio the station for 'assistance escorting someone from town.' After a major stare-down, the men sort of grunted, told Perry they wouldn't forget this, and roared off. I thanked them and drove away as fast as I could!" As an afterthought, she added, "Oh. And we owe him for gas."

"Thank God you're all right!" Madison said, reaching out to clutch the younger woman's hand. "Megan, we have to tell your father about this. I'm sure Otis Perry will make his own report, but he needs to hear it from you. Trust me. This is important."

The auburn-haired girl paled. "You—You don't think these men are the ones he's looking for, do you?"

"I don't know, but they were harassing you. They threatened both you and Perry, and that can't be ignored. Your dad needs to know."

"I—I guess." She released a worried sigh. "I have to admit, it was scary. I'm afraid I may see those men again, and this time, there may not be an officer around to rescue me."

"Maybe they'll heed Perry's words." Madison hoped she sounded more confident than she felt. She doubted the men would scare so easily, not if they were members of a hard-core gang. And certainly not if they were capable of murder.

"Megan, promise me you'll be very, very careful. In fact, it may be a good idea for you to go back to your dorm. You'll be surrounded by people and won't be alone. You'll be safer among numbers."

"But I can't leave you and my dad! What if... what if something terrible happened? I'd never forgive myself."

"And your father would never forgive *him*self if you got tangled up in this mess and ended up hurt," she said gently. Seeing the distress on Megan's face, she squeezed her hand in a gesture of reassurance. "Look. We don't have to decide that right now. Let's talk to your father and see what he says. Right now, let's focus on the here and now. We're here at this fabulous place, and it's all about calm and relaxation. Let's take advantage of that."

"Okay, Mama Maddy. Thanks for listening to me. And, please, don't say anything to my mom, at least not yet."

"I'll agree for now, but she has a right to know, too. She loves you so much. We all do. All we want is to protect you."

"I know. And I appreciate that. But let's keep it between the two of us for today." She forced a brave smile. "And you're right. This place is awesome. Let's just focus on relaxing."

Madison insisted Megan be the next to go in, hoping it helped to relax her. When it was finally her turn, Madison slid into a fluffy robe and stretched face down on a cushioned table. The room was dimly lit and possessed a heady scent that made her sleepy. It was all part of the technique and quite effective. By the time Miss Zuri came in, Madison thought she might purr in contentment.

"Just relax, *ma douce*, and let Miss Zuri ease all your troubles and aches away." With strong yet gentle hands, she worked on Maddy's shoulders and neck. "Is *charmant,* is it not?"

"Very," she murmured in agreement.

As the older woman worked her magic, she hummed. A soft, steady beat of drums began played from the speakers as Miss Zuri mingled more of the strange words from earlier into her melody. Madison knew a spattering of French, but these were different from the simple terms her hostess used in conversation. These had an almost spiritual, reverent quality about them. Soon, the words and the beat of the drums became interwoven, pulsing throughout her body in a steady thrum, pushing their way beneath her skin with each kneaded muscle. Madison had the oddest sensation of being transported into a different world. Almost in a daze, she allowed herself to fully relax for the first time in days.

Miss Zuri continued her lyrical mastery with a mixture of humming, singing, and low, chanted words. Deeply entranced, Maddy only heard a pleasant babble. She didn't want it to ever end.

It did, of course, and soon, the music stopped, and the lights gradually brightened. Madison groaned out a protest, but Miss Zuri only laughed.

"You come again, *ma douce,* and we will work out more of that tightness. You really must learn to *se détendre*. Relax."

"I'll try," she agreed.

As she sat up, Miss Zuri wagged a reprimand with her finger. "Not try. Do."

What a wonderful concept, Madison mused as she dressed. *Don't* try *to relax. Just do.*

Madison was still raving about their visit to the spa that evening. Granny Bert had dropped by to bring fresh-baked cookies, and Madison had insisted she stay for dinner.

Even now, browning ground meat to go into the spaghetti sauce, she looked serene. "It was wonderful,

Granny Bert. You really should go there and see for yourself."

"I'm not much for having other folks' hands all over me," Granny Bert said, eying the way Madison lazily stirred the meat. "You look like you're about to fall asleep just standing there. Maybe you shouldn't be at the stove."

"I'm fine," she insisted with a laugh. "I'm not sleepy. My muscles are a little like pudding, but they'll keep me upright."

"I'm not much on having pudding for muscles, either," her grandmother grumbled. "What's so great about this place that has everyone so starry eyed?"

Madison considered the question before answering. "I think it's the pampering aspect. We all lead such busy lives and don't take enough time for ourselves. For whatever reason, we women had been conditioned to take care of everyone else's needs before our own. That's not always a bad thing, unless it takes a toll on our own health and well-being. It was nice to go in, leave our cares at the door, and just enjoy the peace and pampering."

"I can see the appeal for some, I suppose, but it still doesn't sound like my cup of tea."

"Speaking of tea, in the front, there's a small boutique. She sells teas, spices, bath salts, all kinds of creams and lotions, essence oils, incense, candles... all sorts of things."

"Incense?" She heard the scorn in her grandmother's voice.

"It's not just for hippies anymore, you know," Madison teased.

Granny Bert's reply was a grunted harrumph.

"Seriously, though, you should go at least once. You don't have to get a full massage. You can have a pedicure or just take a look around. Delphine swears by the tea they sell there. She says it's a special blend Miss Zuri makes herself and that it's very calming."

Granny Bert was more interested in Delphine Craddock than she was in the newest store to the area. "Speaking of Delphine, anything new on that front? Has she had any more anger episodes?"

"Oh, my goodness, I forgot to tell you about last night!"

"What about last night? What happened?"

"Brash had a meeting, so Meg and I decided to eat out. As we were coming out, Delphine was going inside with two young men. She introduced them as her grandson and his friend. We were having a friendly little chat when, right out of the blue, I saw a change come over her."

"What kind of change?"

"A very strange one! It was actually kind of spooky. One minute, she was smiling and complimenting Megan on her hair. Less than a minute later, it was like someone flipped a switch." She used hand motions to indicate an explosion. "Her entire demeanor changed. Her eyes went cloudy, her voice came out sharp, and she acted hostile."

Granny Bert paused as she filled a pot for the pasta. "Just like that?"

"Just like that."

"That is strange."

"Even the kids noticed the change in her behavior. Nate pulled up, and Megan went to meet him, which I thought may have been part of it. Her grandson and his friend didn't try hiding their interest in Megan, so I thought maybe Delphine found it rude. I tried soothing things over by mentioning the two of them were seeing one another. Which, now that I think about it, she reacted to rather oddly." A frown tugged at her mouth in retrospect. "She seemed offended that Megan was dating a policeman and kept glaring in their direction. I literally had to step between her and them and squeeze her arm to bring her attention back to me. She was really rattled when I asked if she was having another spell of anger. She admitted to having the anger wash over her, but she couldn't remember how she reacted."

"I agree with the spooky assessment," Granny Bert said.

"The only good thing to come out of it was that she agreed to see a doctor."

"You say she was upset that Megan was dating a cop?"

Madison stirred the meat one last time before she added the spaghetti sauce. "It sure seemed that way."

Taking her time opening the pasta package, Granny Bert was slow to suggest, "Maybe it's time we mention this to Brash. I know that Delphine Craddock seems perfectly harmless, but something's not right with her. You don't just go off like a firecracker for no reason at all. Something's igniting her anger. And if it's the fact that Megan is dating a cop..."

Another recollection deepened Madison's frown. "Her grandson mentioned meeting Brash earlier in the day. Apparently, he offered the boys a ride, and Delphine made some snide remark about it being to the jail. The venom in her voice surprised even the grandson."

"Does he have a record?"

"I have no idea. She seemed suspicious of Brash's intentions, though, so maybe that's it."

"Maybe that's why she didn't like the idea of Megan dating Nate. Maybe her grandson's had run-ins with the law before," Granny Bert rationalized.

"That makes sense, I suppose. I know—"

Before she could finish her sentence, Megan

clamored down the back stairs, her voice frantic.

"Mama Maddy! Hurry! We have to go! We have to go now!"

"What? What is it, sweetie?" Madison asked, seeing tears streaking down Megan's pale face. "What's happened?"

"Nate's been hurt! He's at the ER!"

16

Brash was already at Texas General Hospital in College Station when the women arrived. "We still don't have a lot of details, sweetheart," he told his daughter.

"What happened, though? Is he—Is he going to be all right?"

"They haven't given me an update on his condition since I called you, but they've given me no reason to believe it's life threatening."

"Oh, thank God," Megan said, slumping against him.

"What else can you tell us, Brash?" Madison asked.

"Not much, I'm afraid. The doctor says he came in contact with some type of poison, but—"

Megan gasped. "Poison?" she asked in an incredulous voice.

Her father nodded. "Apparently so."

"Where on earth did he come into contact with poison?" Madison asked. "What kind was it?"

"They don't know. It will take a series of tests and a complete blood analysis to narrow down the general class of poison used. Even more tests to know the precise compound."

"That's crazy!" Megan protested. "Nate is very cautious. He knows not to handle poison with his bare hands. At the very least, he would wear gloves."

"He may not have handled it. He could have ingested it," her father pointed out.

Megan's forehead crinkled. "I know he called in an order at *Montelongo's* for dinner last night. Maddy and I ate there, too, and neither of us are sick."

"I suppose someone could have slipped it into his order specifically, knowing he was a police officer," Madison spoke her thoughts aloud. "But it would have to contain a slow-acting agent, or he would have been sick long before now."

Brash groaned as a thought occurred to him.

Madison read the expression on his face. "What?" she asked in alarm.

He was already punching numbers into his phone. As soon as the line picked up, he rushed to say, "Vina! Are those brownies still in the break room?"

"You mean the ones clumsy Otis Perry knocked into the trashcan? Nate was the only one to even get one. The rest were destroyed."

Brash blew out a relieved breath. "For once, his clumsiness may have been a good thing," he told her. "Salvage what you can and put them aside. Do not let *anyone* taste them."

Her reply was a confused, "Oh-kay..."

"And be sure to wear gloves when handling them," he warned.

"Brash, what is going on? What's wrong with those brownies?"

"The doctors say Nate was poisoned. The brownies may have nothing to do with it, but they were delivered anonymously this afternoon. I should have questioned it at the time," he said in guilty retrospect.

"Why? It's not unusual for people to drop off sweets

at the station. Sybil does it all the time. It's a show of appreciation."

"Unless it's not."

Vina sucked in a sharp breath. "You think that's where Nate ingested the poison? Someone brazenly brought it into the station?"

"It's worth checking out. Put the brownies in a bag and don't let anyone near them. I'll send them to the lab for analysis."

"I'd better hurry, before the trash runs."

"Go. I'll check in later."

Madison watched him hang up. "What was that all about?"

"Someone dropped off a batch of brownies this afternoon at the station. Nate grabbed one on his way out for patrol. Apparently, Perry came along and knocked the rest into the trash, so no one else was able to eat any."

Madison followed his train of thought. "And then Nate came down sick."

"Right. It may be nothing, but then again, it may be something."

"Who brought the brownies?"

"No one remembers seeing anyone bringing them in. They were just there beside the coffeepot, and Nate helped himself to one." Brash rubbed a hand over his weary face. "I should have questioned it. I should have been more cautious."

"You had no way of knowing they could have been laced with poison, Daddy," Megan assured him. "*If* that's what happened. We still don't know anything for certain."

"No, but here comes his doctor. Maybe she has some good news for us."

After introductions were made, Doctor Sherwood offered what news she had. "Deputy Stone is alert and gave verbal permission for us to speak with you regarding his medical status," she said first off. "The good news is he didn't ingest enough of the poison to do serious damage to any vital organs. None of the effects should be permanent, but the downside is that they have weakened his muscles, and he's still a bit disoriented. I want to keep him overnight to monitor his condition and reevaluate in the morning. Maybe by then we'll have identified the agent and be in a better position as to how to treat him. We're thinking it could be organophosphate poisoning but it's too soon to say."

"Like used in farming and agriculture?" Brash asked. "Wouldn't he have tasted it?"

"Not in small quantities, and not if there were strong enough flavors in the food or drink he consumed. Again, we're not certain that was the agent, but it's certainly on our radar." She looked at Brash and warned, "I advise that he be put on light duty for at least three to five days. He didn't take the news well, saying something about a public safety matter within the county, but I must think of his own safety. Ideally, I would suggest he take time off to rest, but he insists this is an emergency situation. I'll allow light duty behind a desk, but whether he realizes it or not, his stamina will be affected. His body needs time to recuperate and heal in order for his muscles to strengthen properly. If it is OP poisoning, a full recovery requires resynthesis of new enzyme, a process that takes several weeks."

"Absolutely, Doctor," Brash readily agreed. "I'll see to it that your orders are followed."

"Very well." With a smile, Dr. Sherwood turned to Megan. "You must be Megan, the beautiful redhead the deputy spoke of."

Blushing, her reply was a murmured affirmation. "I'm Megan."

"In that case, I'll escort you back to see our patient." Her eyes danced with playfulness. "He requested to see you first, before the interrogation from his boss." She threw a glance at the chief, putting her hands up in a gesture of innocence. "His words, not mine. Come with me, Megan."

Megan cringed at the sights and sounds accosting her as they strode to the rear of the emergency department. A baby wailed in distress. Call buttons dinged a steady tune of need. From behind their cubicles, patients moaned and begged for relief. Someone pushed a gurney down the corridor, trailed by spots of blood. A nervous energy hummed in the air, punctuated with pain and suffering.

Was the doctor downplaying Nate's condition? Megan worried. If he was here among the gloom and the hurting, was he worse than the pretty doctor claimed?

"I'll give you a few minutes alone," Dr. Sherwood said, showing her to the room. "He's still weak, so try not to tire him."

"I won't," she promised.

Megan's fears were somewhat alleviated when she saw Nate propped up against his pillow and wearing a weak smile.

"You came," he said.

"Of course I came!" Megan rushed toward his bed. "How could I not? I was so worried! How are you?"

Nate caught hold of her hand. "Better, now that you're here."

The two hadn't been dating for long. Their relationship was still new and uncertain, but Megan felt no hesitation as she reached out with the other hand and brushed the hair away from his forehead. Her fingers lingered in the dark threads, and she dared stroke the rest as she studied his face for signs of distress.

Nate's face was pale and drawn, but his blue eyes were bright. He watched her watch him as his hold on her hand tightened.

"What happened, Nate?" Megan's eyes clouded with worry.

"I don't know. One minute, I was walking toward the front door; the next, I was on the floor, writhing in pain. My stomach was cramping like never before, and I broke out in a cold sweat. Then I started puking and couldn't stop. Things got a little fuzzy after that. I was in so much pain and so weak. Vina called the ambulance, and I ended up in here." Even his shrug looked perplexed.

"I'm just glad it happened in the office, where someone was nearby to help! What if... what if it had happened at home when you were all alone?" She shivered just thinking about it.

"I know. I thought the same thing," he told her solemnly.

"The doctor said she wants to keep you overnight." When a scowl darkened his face, Megan gave him a chastising look. "Please don't be stubborn and insist you're all right."

A hint of his old self twinkled in his eye as he pretended an affront. "You think I'm stubborn?"

"I *know* you're stubborn. But I'm serious, Nate. You need to stay here and let them watch you for any lingering side effects."

"If I was strong enough to protest, I would," he admitted. "But for once, I don't think I have it in me. I'm not sure I could walk out of here without help."

"I hate to say this, but good. That way I don't have to tie you to this bed."

"I don't want you worrying about me, Meg. I'll be okay."

"I can't help but worry, Nate." Megan caught her lower lip in her teeth, suddenly shy. "I've been frantic, thinking the worst..."

"Megan." His voice, still weak, took on a new reserve. His words came out deeper, and more solemn. "I know they'll probably run you out soon, and I know your dad still needs to talk to me. But there's something I have to tell you."

Her heart stilled, uncertain of what he might say.

"They say it takes something traumatic to make you appreciate the things that are important in your life, and after today, I think being poisoned rates as traumatic enough." His eyes dropped as he concentrated on intertwining his fingers with hers. "I had an idea this was happening, but now I'm certain." His gaze sought hers. "I have feelings for you, Megan. Strong feelings. When I get out of here, I'd like to see where that takes us. If... If that's what you want, of course."

"Yes!" She squeezed his fingers with watering eyes and a happy smile. "Yes, that's absolutely what I want."

"I'd love nothing more than to kiss you right now," he whispered, watching her bat away tears, "but I don't know if it's safe. I don't know if there's any residual poison left in my system."

From behind them, an amused voice spoke. Neither had heard the nurse come in. "There's not. And you've brushed your teeth," she teased, "so I see no reason why you shouldn't be able to kiss your girlfriend."

Megan blushed furiously, but Nate had no such qualms. "I like the sound of that. My girlfriend." He tugged her forward until Megan leaned across him. Fisting his hand in her hair, he used what little strength he had to hold her close and kiss her. The kiss wasn't deep, but it held promise.

For now, that was enough.

"I'm sorry, Megan," family friend Nurse Laurel Benson said, "but we need to let Nate rest for a moment before your dad questions him."

Laurel's own boyfriend was a local detective, and more often than not, they clashed over the patient's needs versus the need for a speedy interrogation. She knew time was always of the essence when investigating a crime, but her unfailing allegiance was to her patient. Keeping them healthy and cared for was her top priority.

"I understand," Megan murmured. She gave Nate one last peck on the lips. "Do what Laurel says. Believe me, you don't want to cross that little stick of dynamite."

"For you, anything," the deputy agreed. He released her hand with reluctance.

"Once you're settled in a room upstairs," the nurse assured him, "Megan can visit longer. Take a few minutes to rest and collect your strength. I'll bring Br— Chief deCordova—back in a few minutes."

Leading Megan back through the maze of hallways, Laurel smiled and said, "He seems like a very good man. I'm happy for you, Megan."

"He is. We haven't been seeing each other for very long, but we just clicked, you know?"

Laurel couldn't help but laugh. "I've heard it can happen that way, but it wasn't at all like that for Cade and me. We were at odds, right from the beginning. Sometimes, I think we still are, but something keeps pulling us back together."

"Fate?" Megan mused.

"Something like that. It certainly keeps things interesting. How's your dad feel about you dating another cop?"

"He wants me to be happy, of course, but I have a feeling he wishes I had fallen for someone in a different line of work, especially now." There was no mistaking the worry in her voice.

"I've heard about the problems you're having in River County. It seems crazy for something like that to happen there."

"It's crazy for it to happen anywhere," Megan countered. "Why people hate the police so much is beyond me. I know there are bad cops out there, just like there are bad criminals. But you can't assume it's all of them. Not all cops are bad. Not all people are crooks. There's no blanket that covers them all into one bed."

"Well said. And I agree wholeheartedly." She pressed the button to open the wide set of doors. "I'll be out to call your dad in about ten minutes. Nate is still very weak and needs his rest."

"Thanks for taking such good care of him."

"Of course. And try not to worry so much. I think he'll make a full recovery and be back to his old self in no time." Laurel gave the younger woman a brief hug. "Oops. They're calling for me. Gotta go."

Caught up with another patient, it was closer to fifteen minutes later when Laurel had a chance to fetch Brash.

Another fifteen minutes, and he was back out in the waiting room.

"Did he remember anything helpful?" Madison asked.

"Not particularly. He confirmed he had eaten one of the brownies someone left. He said it was very good, but it had a slight taste he didn't recognize. It went through his mind that someone may have laced it with marijuana as some sort of joke. Or even a laxative, like his roommates did in college. It never occurred to him that they could have used something more dangerous." Brash ran a weary hand over his face, still coming to terms that someone possibly brought a dangerous substance into the station, and they hadn't even known it.

"It must have been an extremely fast-acting poison," Madison observed.

"As it turns out, he didn't go straight out the door as we first believed. Someone called the station, asking for him. It was several minutes before he actually made for the door, until excruciating pain set in and stopped him in his tracks."

"I'm just glad it happened in the station, rather than on the road. Especially if he had been driving!"

Listening to her parents talk, Megan hugged her arms around herself. "I know it could be a long night," she said, "and I know you both need to get back home. Mama Maddy, why don't you ride with Daddy and leave the car with me? I'd like to know Nate was settled into a room before I go home."

Brash frowned. "There's no telling when that may be. I don't like the idea of you driving in the middle of the night."

"Then I'll sleep in the waiting room or in a chair in his room."

"Maybe Laurel could put you up for the night," Madison suggested.

"I'll figure something out. You two go on, try to get some rest, and I'll stay here and keep an eye on Nate."

With some reluctance from her parents, the matter was settled. As they walked out to Brash's department-issued SUV, Madison slipped her hand into his.

"It just keeps getting worse, doesn't it?" she whispered.

"We're going to find these SOBs." Brash's jaw was set in determination. "One way or another, we're going to find them and shut them down."

Madison shivered. When her husband got that look

in his eyes and that tone in his voice, there was no stopping him. *But at what cost?*

It was a thought that haunted her throughout the night.

17

After a restless night and three cups of coffee, Madison managed a chipper voice as she answered the phone. As usual, Derron was late coming in.

"*In a Pinch.* This is Madison. May I help you?"

"Madison? This is Tammy Bishop."

"Oh, hello, Tammy. How are you today?"

"I've been better. I fell and twisted my ankle, and the doctor's told me to stay off it for a few days. That's why I'm calling. I know it's short notice, but is there *any* way you could squeeze me in your schedule?"

"I imagine I could do that. What days?"

Tammy released a huffed breath. "Today would be better, but I'll settle for the rest of the week. Do you think you can do it?"

"What are your hours?"

"Ten to five. I close at two on Saturday."

Madison glanced at her watch. "It's a quarter till nine. I think I could manage today, as well."

"Really? That would be awesome!"

"I'll need to get the key. And a few details, of course. Like how to use your cash register."

"I don't have anything fancy. Just a regular old register; punch in a price and hit total."

"That sounds easy enough. And the key?"

"The one thing I do have is a fancy lock with an access code. Use Juliet's zip code, and you should be able to get right in. If you have any problems, just call me."

"Any special instructions once I'm in?"

Tammy went through a brief tutorial of where the light switches were, where she kept bags and tissue paper, what ambiance lighting she used, and a few other minor details.

"You have no idea how much I appreciate this, Madison!" Tammy said in sincerity. "I don't have a very big gift shop, and some days I only have a few sales, but I hate to close unnecessarily. You stepping in for me is a huge deal."

"My pleasure, Tammy. I always enjoy going into your shop, so it really won't feel like work. In fact, I'll probably have trouble not shopping for myself!" she admitted with a laugh.

"Then take an extra ten percent employee discount off."

"I couldn't do that!"

"I usually hire extra help at the holidays, and that's one of the perks I offer. You're squeezing me in at the last moment, so it's the least I can do!"

"I don't mind at all. Will you be home in case I have to call and ask questions?"

"The doctor left me strict instructions to plant myself on the couch, elevate my leg, and keep an ice pack on my ankle. So, yes, I'll be home." She sounded none too pleased about it.

"Just take care of yourself, and I'll take care of the store."

"Thanks again, Madison."

"No problem, Tammy. Enjoy the down time." As she hung up, Madison was already jotting Derron a note about her change in plans.

An hour later, she let herself into the back door of *Tammy's Treasures* and flipped light switches. As the storeroom and the shop beyond flooded with light, Madison went in to familiarize herself with the merchandise and where everything was located. By the time she turned over the 'Open' sign, she felt optimistic about the day to come.

The little store had more traffic than she had expected. She wasn't exactly busy, and not everyone left with a purchase, but there were several people who came in and browsed. Occasionally, one of them bought something, and Madison would happily bag their purchases.

All of her customers for the day were women, except for one man who came in late that afternoon.

"May I help you?" she offered.

"Nah. Just looking." He looked uncomfortable, surrounded by breakable nicknacks, flowered stationary items, and women's shirts, scarves, and jewelry.

"No problem. Just let me know if you need help selecting anything."

Madison wandered back to the checkout counter, where she looked over the notes she had made. One woman wanted Tammy to re-order an item she had seen there last week, another was looking for a particular blouse in a different color, and one teenager was inquiring about help during the holidays.

After meticulously browsing through the store, the man brought a necklace to the register. "I think I'll surprise my wife and give her this." He presented the leather rawhide string with its arrow charm. "She's into archery, so I thought she might get a kick out of this."

"That's very thoughtful of you," Madison said with a smile. "Would you like that gift wrapped?"

"You don't have to do that. She's just next door at that essentials place. I've been killing time while she gets... whatever it is that she gets." He looked rather clueless as to what his wife did in a spa. "I'll just give it to her when she gets out."

"At least it'll be in a cute bag with some tissue paper."

Madison rang up the purchase and handed him his bag. "I hope your wife enjoys her gift."

"I'm sure she will. She's a member of the Archery Club in Riverton. She has those decorative arrows and stuff all over the house."

"Then I'm sure you made an excellent choice." Madison smiled at him. "Come back and see us."

"I don't usually drive her, but I did this time. She somehow twisted her ankle the other night."

"Really? That's the same thing that happened to the owner of this store. I'm just filling in for her today."

"Let's hope it's not contagious! I've got too much to do to be down with a sprained ankle."

"Luckily, I don't think those sorts of things are contagious. Just an inconvenience to those suffering."

The man scrunched his nose. "And for the husbands who have to cart them around to their frou-frou places."

Madison laughed as the man left the shop. He pretended to be aggravated with his wife, but the thoughtful gift in his hand begged to differ.

Since she hadn't been prepared for this spur-of-the-moment job, Madison called in an order to *New Beginnings* and took hamburgers home for dinner.

It was just she and Brash sitting down to eat. Nate was being released from the hospital, and Megan was his ride back to Juliet. She had spent the night by his side, come home to freshen up, and was now off to College Station again.

Young love, Madison mused.

"What's with the smile?" Brash asked. "That good of a day?"

"It actually was a good day," she replied. "Some of the jobs I take are boring, just sitting around answering the phone or waiting for a customer to come in. But Tammy has a steady clientele, and the day flew by."

"Sell a lot?"

"Not really, but it was fun. About half of the people just came in to browse, but that's okay. They may come back another day and buy the store out." At his arched brow, she amended, "Okay, maybe not buy the store out. But they might buy *something,* and that's better than nothing."

Brash gave a convincingly somber nod. "Sage observation, my dear."

"What about you? How was your day? The fact that you're down one officer and still home for dinner is surprising."

"I'm on call with the fire department, so that could change at any moment. As for my day... I spent most of it trying to chase down who brought the brownies."

His heavy tone suggested defeat. "No luck?" Madison asked sympathetically.

"Not yet."

"Anything new on the investigation?"

"Not that I'm aware of. I notified the other departments about Nate's poisoning, but no one reported any similar incidents. On the upside, however, River County Deputy Clemens is much better."

"Does he remember anything about his attack?"

"One thing, but Sheriff Larson wasn't sure it meant anything. Just before being hit on the head, Clemens got a whiff of something. Not cologne, but something sweet. He said it was hard to describe, but he swears he had smelt it before."

"Chloroform?"

"It would make sense if his attacker planned to knock him out with a dosed handkerchief, but that's been ruled out."

"Marijuana?" she suggested.

"He said not. He said it had an earthy scent to it, but yet sweet." His broad shoulders lifted in a shrug. "For all we know, it was a flower. It may or may not mean a thing."

"That doesn't sound too helpful," she agreed, popping a french fry in her mouth.

"So far, nothing has proved helpful."

Glancing down at his empty hamburger wrapper, Madison teased, "At least your appetite hasn't been affected."

"I've got to keep up my strength."

"Then it's a good thing I ordered Genny's famous apple turnovers for dessert." Not only were they delicious, but it might be a good way to sweeten her husband up while she told him about Delphine Craddock. "How 'bout I pop them in the microwave and add a scoop of vanilla ice cream?"

His lips lifted in a smile, something Madison rarely saw these days. "It sounds delicious, but I'll get it. You're still eating."

When Madison's phone rang, she wiped her fingers on a napkin and swiped the screen. She saw Miss Wanda's name pop up.

"Hello?"

"Madison!" The older woman's voice sounded frantic. "Help me! I—I think someone's shooting at me!"

"What?" Madison was already on her feet, waving at Brash to come closer. She put the call on speakerphone so they could both hear. "Where are you? Are you hurt?"

"I'm in my car outside the grocery store. I—I saw that biker gang, and I think they shot at me!"

Brash spoke over Madison's shoulder. "I'm on my way!"

"Stay calm, Miss Wanda. We'll be there as quick as we can!" Madison assured her.

Brash buckled his service belt around his waist as Madison jerked the kitchen door open. "Where do you think you're going?" he barked.

"With you. And don't argue, because I'm going!"

To her surprise, he didn't say another word. He radioed the station with the report of a possible shooting as the two of them climbed into his SUV.

"Why did she call you and not 9-1-1?" he grumbled, hitting the overhead lights. "You don't need to interfere in a police matter."

"Interfere? She called *me*," she reminded him. "How could I not go?"

"She should have called 9-1-1." His lips pressed together in an angry line.

"It's Wanda Shanks we're talking about. When has she ever done what she should?"

"This isn't funny, Madison. It's bad enough that Megan had a run-in with these men. Now you, too?"

"If they shot at her, I'm sure they're long gone. Which brings up the question of *why* would a motorcycle gang shoot at a sweet old lady like Miss Wanda?"

"Maybe that *sweet* little lady shot them the bird or argued with them over the last bottle of margarita mix."

Madison winced, knowing either was a possibility.

They careened into the parking lot of the grocery store, bouncing over a curb. Madison grabbed the dash with one hand and pointed with the other.

"There's her car!"

"The motorcycles are long gone." He frowned, even though it was no surprise. What *was* a surprise was the relatively empty parking lot. He had expected to see half the town there.

He braked hard as he pulled in behind her car. "Stay here," he told his wife.

Madison glared at him as she opened her door and hopped out. She beat him to Miss Wanda's car by mere seconds. "She's lying across the steering wheel, Brash! I think she's hurt!"

Miss Wanda's ashen face was turned toward them, her puffy cheek pressed against the wheel. Brash pulled her door open, carefully assessing the situation. He could see no blood. No shattered windows. *Where had the shots come from?* He wondered. His keen eyes swept across the parking lot.

"Miss Wanda! Are you okay?" he asked.

"I—I don't think so," she said in a shaky voice.

"Where were you hit?"

"The first bullet missed. But—But the second one got me." Her arm shook as she lifted her right hand to touch the back of her head. She gingerly touched the spot in question. Terrified, she blurted out, "I can feel my brains, Brash! They're falling out. Those men... They shot me in the head!"

Madison gasped, horrified at the words. She was also perplexed. There was no blood, and Miss Wanda was still able to talk. How could that be, with a head injury of that caliber? Wouldn't a shot like that be fatal?

Brash's dark eyes narrowed as the same thoughts raced through his mind. Madison saw him glance into the backseat before peering over the prone woman to the seat beside her. She noticed how his shoulders relaxed, and his whole demeanor changed. He even fought back a smile.

Squatting down beside the older woman, he spoke

in a gentle voice to assure her, "Miss Wanda, you're going to be okay. I don't think you were shot."

"Then—Then what's that glob behind my head? It-It feels like my brains!"

"Did you put your grocery bags in the car, Miss Wanda? They're scattered all over the place."

"I was getting away from those horrid men! I even sat on my bread and squashed it."

"I don't think that's all you squashed." His lip twitched as he reached out to touch the back of her head. "Did you buy biscuits?" he asked.

"Y-Yes. Why?"

He pulled away the offending glob and showed it to her. When her face puckered in confusion, he explained, "It's biscuit dough, Miss Wanda. You must have sat on one of the cans, and it burst open. The force shot a biscuit out, and it hit you in the head."

"A biscuit? Not my brains?" she asked in wonder.

"Not your brains, Miss Wanda. You're fine."

She stared at him for a moment in stunned silence. Then she lifted her head and broke out in a deep belly laugh. "A-A biscuit!" she hooted. "I was shot by a biscuit!" She slapped the steering wheel so hard, the horn beeped.

Joyously, she hit it in three more short bleeps, as if she were clapping. "Oh, this is the funniest thing yet!"

She laughed so hard, tears streamed down her face. Madison and Brash couldn't help but join in. People stepped from the store and from their cars, to stare at the spectacle. It was a strange sight, seeing the red and blue lights flashing. Instead of a frown, the chief of police was crouched beside a car, laughing along with his wife and a woman inside the car. Once they realized the woman was Wanda Shanks, they shrugged their shoulders and went about their business. With her, it was no telling what had happened.

"I can't—I can't believe I thought I was shot!" Wanda squealed, once she caught her breath. "Or that I thought my brains were falling out!" That sent her into another fit of hilarious laughter.

Madison laughed with her. "Oh, Miss Wanda! You had us so worried!"

When the laughter finally subdued, Brash had questions to ask. His first was, "Why did you call Madison and not 9-1-1?"

"She was the first one I thought of!"

In a Wanda Shanks kind of way, it made sense. Brash moved on to a more pressing issue. "What about the men on the motorcycles? What happened with them?"

"Well," she huffed, "it started in the produce aisle. I popped a grape into my mouth—okay, maybe a whole stem—just to make sure they were sweet and tasty. There were two men there, dressed in leathers and tattoos. Rough-looking men, they were. One said I shouldn't be sampling the goods, and I told him to mind his own business. His face turned all dark, and his friend started to say something mean. So, I popped a grape into his mouth to shut him up. Next thing I know, they're eating the whole bunch. I saw my chance to get away, and I took it! But then they showed up at the register behind me, and one asked if I was going to steal any more groceries. I said, 'not as many as you did.' His friend laughed, which didn't make him happy. I paid the cashier and hurried out before she could ring up their case of beer. I shoved my bags inside, just as they came out the door. I knew I was sitting on the bread. but that was the least of my worries. I hoped they wouldn't see me, but when they got on their bikes, one of them looked me straight in the eye. That's when I heard the first shot. I immediately called Madison. And then—" She broke out in laughter again. "Then I heard the second shot, which wasn't a shot at all! I must have sat on the roll of biscuits, popped it open, and sent the biscuits flying!" She threw back her head and bellowed out a loud laugh. "Just wait until I tell the girls!" She clapped her hands together in glee, just imagining their responses.

"Oh, Miss Wanda, you are a jewel!" Madison impulsively hugged the rotund woman.

"I'm sorry to cause all the ruckus," she apologized. "I really thought I was a goner."

"It could have happened to anyone," Brash smoothly lied.

Miss Wanda clutched Maddy's arm as an idea occurred to her. "Don't tell Derron about this! I can wrap my head with gauze and tell him my story. Can you imagine his face when I tell him my brains were hanging out of my head? He'll turn as white as a ghost and maybe even faint!" She laughed again, lost in her own musings.

As Brash crawled back into the truck and killed the strobe lights, he shook his head in amazement. "That woman," was all he said, but the two words said it all.

"Bless her heart," Madison agreed. "She really was terrified when we arrived. She truly thought she had been shot and that her brains..." She fought another chuckle, knowing it was a serious yet hilarious situation.

"The worst part of the whole thing is knowing the motorcycle gang is back in town. They openly ignored Perry's warning, and they're harassing people."

Madison looked skeptical. "Miss Wanda is as bad as my grandmother, you know," she pointed out. "Neither of them can keep quiet, even in dangerous situations. I'm not sure the men are completely to blame on this one."

His look remained like stone. "They are if they disobeyed an order not to come back to The Sisters."

18

Granny Bert visited *Tammy's Treasures* the next day to supposedly 'keep Madison company.' Her granddaughter saw through the ruse, knowing Granny Bert was eager to tell Wanda's story to anyone who would listen. She employed her usual dramatic flair, leaving her listeners spellbound with hushed breath. No matter how many times she told the story, she laughed along with them.

In truth, Madison laughed, too, but she tried hiding it. She felt bad about finding humor in Miss Wanda's very real fear, until she discovered the other woman was telling her story with even more relish than Granny Bert. After that, Madison didn't bother covering her laugh. It *was* a funny story, after all.

The jovial spirit in the room was good for sales. Not only did more people buy, but they also sent their friends in, too. Rather than relay the story themselves, they encouraged their friends to visit the shop and hear Granny Bert's lively rendition of events. While Granny Bert told the story on repeat, Madison steadily rang up sales.

By mid-afternoon, Madison was exhausted. "I should tell you to visit the store more often, but I'm not sure Tammy could keep up! We practically sold out of candles and melts today!"

"What can I say?" the older woman grinned. "People love a good story, especially when it's told by a great storyteller."

The bell jingled above the door, and Miss Sybil walked in.

"Hello, Miss Sybil. How are you?" Madison asked with a smile.

"Very well, thank you. I just came from next door, and Miss Zuri worked wonders on my tired legs." She turned shrewd eyes on her best friend. "You really should go in there, Bertha. The woman is a magician. She gives a wonderful massage. By the time she slathers you with lotion, you're so relaxed, you can hardly walk."

Granny Bert snorted. "You seem steady enough on your feet."

Her friend smiled. "That's because I sat long enough to sip a cup of tea. It rejuvenated me!"

"I'm glad you like it, but that sort of thing's just not for me."

"What kind of thing?" Sybil almost looked offended.

"Voodoo and what not."

"I've told you a hundred times, it's not voodoo!" she snapped.

"Okay. Swamp witch legends, then. Just because the woman is Cajun and wears a turban doesn't mean she can cast spells."

"They're not spells; they're tried and true methods. Even a nurse from Riverton goes there. She works for a holistic doctor and says Miss Zuri's methods are completely safe and known to be beneficial. She uses only natural ingredients that she mixes into lotions and teas. Incense, too."

"Potions," Granny Bert insisted.

"If you're going to insult me, I'm leaving," Sybil said.

"What's gotten into you, Sybil? To be so relaxed, you sure are twitchy."

Her friend sniffed in displeasure. "I just don't like you ridiculing something I happen to like and enjoy."

"Fair enough," Granny Bert conceded. "I'll try not to express my thoughts on the subject if you agree to keep your ravings down to a mild roar."

Sybil glared at her oldest and dearest friend. "I mean it, Bertha Hamilton Cessna! One more wisecrack, and I'm leaving."

Madison broke into their argument. "Miss Sybil, have you heard what happened to Miss Wanda last night?"

"They were talking about it next door. I heard she was surrounded by a motorcycle gang, and they tried to steal her car. I haven't had a chance to call her yet and check in on her."

"That's not what happened. Here, let Granny Bert tell you the story."

Granny Bert launched into her rendition of the tale, which had all three women laughing once again. Just when Madison thought things were back to normal, Miss Sybil made a sudden turnabout.

"I'm glad she called Madison, and not that no-good-for-nothing 9-1-1."

Madison couldn't help a small gasp of surprise. "Miss Sybil! Why would you say such a thing?"

"It's true," she insisted. "The operators don't give people a chance. They tell the officers a crime has been committed, even before it's confirmed. The officers go in prejudiced, assuming the worse about the so-called suspect."

"That's not true. 9-1-1 is for all kinds of emergencies, not just crimes. It's used to report fires, accidents, disabled vehicles, loose livestock... all sorts of things that could easily become a problem, or even life threatening. 9-1-1 is a valuable asset to the community."

"Spoken like a cop's wife!"

Madison stared at the woman in disbelief. She had always considered Miss Sybil more of an aunt than her grandmother's friend, and she was quite fond of her. The venom in her voice shocked Madison. Dismayed, she said, "I—I don't know what to say, Miss Sybil. I've never seen you like this before."

"Like what?"

Biting her tongue, Madison just murmured a hasty "excuse me" and retreated to the storeroom.

"What got into her?" Sybil asked.

"You!" Granny Bert told her in no uncertain terms. "Why would you attack Madison, of all people? And Brash? I thought you like both of them!"

"I do, but I don't trust the police, and Brash happens to be a policeman."

Granny Bert narrowed her eyes. "Since when don't you trust the police?"

"Never you mind. I think it's just best I go now."

"So do I!" She stalked to the door and opened it, speeding her friend's exit along.

Madison peeked around the corner. "Is she gone?"

"Yes, and it's a good thing! I could have said something I regretted."

"What's wrong with her, Granny? Is she having some sort of breakdown? A break from reality?"

Granny Bert squinted at the closed door. "I don't know, girl, but I think it's time I call her son and tell him what's going on with his momma."

After her grandmother left, Madison rearranged empty spaces on the shelves. She made notes for Tammy on what to reorder. Just before closing, the bell jingled again, and another familiar face came through the door.

"Miss Delphine. How are you today?"

Noticing the duster in Madison's hand, she asked, "Madison? Are you working here now?"

"Just temping. Tammy sprained her ankle, so she called me to help out for a few days."

"Oh, that's nice. Not that she sprained her ankle, of course, but that you could help."

"That's what I do. Help people when they're in a pinch. Now, on behalf of Tammy... How may I help you?"

"I still need that gift for my niece. I saw a nice bracelet in here, so I thought I'd come back and get it."

"Wonderful. What did it look like?"

"It was a silver bracelet with a single charm, a cute little seashell. I know Amy likes the beach, so I think it would be perfect for her. It was more than I wanted to spend, but I haven't found anything else that suited me."

"Oh dear. I'm afraid I sold that one this morning, and there weren't any more in the storeroom. Maybe we can find something else she would like."

"I don't know what. I'm at my wit's end trying to find something!"

"I'm sure we can find something. How old is she?"

"Fifteen."

Madison thought it over for a moment. "At that age, clothes are probably out of the question, unless you know exactly the style she likes. Most teenagers think we don't know a thing about fashion."

"Judging by the holey jeans they wear these days, I tend to agree," Delphine sighed. "I wouldn't dare let my children leave the house like that! I patched all their jeans when they got holes in them."

"I know," Madison laughed. "Styles have certainly

changed!" They were near a display of mixes and bakewear. "Does she like to cook?"

"Actually, she does. She especially likes to bake."

The infamous brownies came to mind. Madison dared to ask, "Is that something she got from you?"

Delphine brushed away the thought with a small laugh. "Heavens, no! I burn anything that goes into the oven. I can cook on the range top with the best of them, but baking just isn't my thing."

"Okay," Madison said, somewhat relieved. "What about a cookbook? Or maybe this cute little skillet with a packet of cookie mix and a spatula? Does that look like something she would like?"

"I think it might be," the other woman nodded. "Thank you, Madison. What a wonderful suggestion! I would have never thought of it myself."

"Certainly. Would you like it gift wrapped?"

"Even better. Being as I'm still getting settled in, I have no idea where my gift-wrapping supplies are."

"Then give me a minute, and I'll have this ready for you."

Delphine roamed the store, while Madison found a box and paper to wrap the present. Delphine brought a birthday card to the register and told her to add it to the bill.

"How are you doing, Delphine?" Madison asked as she put the finishing touches on the box. "Any more issues?"

"Not really. I felt a brief surge of anger earlier, while I was waiting to get my massage. But it passed quickly, and I seem to be fine now."

"I knew you bought tea from Miss Zuri, but I didn't know if you used her services. I had my first massage from her this week. It was wonderful."

"Isn't it, though?"

"Those lotions smell and feel fantastic. My skin still

feels dewy."

"I know what you mean," Delphine said with a dreamy expression. "And that music she plays is so relaxing. I have no idea what they're saying, but it soothes me. Makes me feel almost like I'm floating."

"The whole experience was amazing. And what's even more amazing is that she does all the massages herself. With as many people as I saw coming and going, I don't know how she manages it all by herself."

"If you noticed, her staff does everything else, while she does the massages. It seems to work well."

"Yes, I agree." Madison presented the gaily wrapped box. "Is this okay?"

"It's lovely! I think she'll be so pleased."

"I'm glad you like it."

"Thank you, Madison. Not just for this, but for everything."

"I'm happy to help. If anything else happens, please, don't hesitate to call me."

"I won't. You really helped me last time I called. I hope there won't be any more instances, but I guess it's too soon to tell. I'll be in touch."

As Madison locked up the shop, Brash and Deputy Schimanski were still on patrol. While looking for any signs of trouble, they kept a sharp eye out for the men on motorcycles. They saw nothing alarming on their round but when the radio crackled with a call, they sat up straighter in their seats.

"SO to all departments. We have reports of a robbery at 417 Taylor Road in Low Crossing. One injury reported. Be on the lookout for a dark-blue Camaro with racing stripes. Two male suspects, one Caucasian, one Hispanic. Assailants are assumed to be armed and dangerous and should not be approached without proper backup."

A second tone-out immediately followed. "SO to River County EMS 3. We have a 42-year-old white male with unknown injuries at 417 Taylor Road in Low Crossing."

Schimanski looked over at his boss. "Didn't you say witnesses reported a Camaro riding with that motorcycle gang the night before Robles died?"

"Yes. They described it as dark, unsure of exact color, and souped up."

"Do you think this is the car?"

"The description seems to fit. So do the descriptions of the suspects. But neither are enough to assume these are the same guys."

"But it's worth considering, don't you think?"

"Absolutely. We'll make a few more rounds on the blacktop roads, particularly FM 903 that runs toward Low Crossing."

Keeping their eyes sharp, they drove west toward the small town of Low Crossing. The Camaro could have taken the highway east out of town and turned onto the farm-to-market road. If so, their paths would meet.

"Do you think these guys are the ones behind the attacks?" Schmanski asked.

"I don't know." Brash wore a frown. "A robbery doesn't fit their MO. So far, the attacks have been on first responders. Why shift to robbery?"

"Maybe to throw us off track?"

"Possibly."

"You don't sound convinced."

"The only thing I'm convinced of is that we need to find the perpetrators and shut them down before anyone else has been hurt."

"I hear ya, boss."

They drove around for another hour without seeing signs of the blue sports car. Calling it a day, they returned to the station.

Once there, Brash disappeared to his office. He called area departments and reminded them that a car matching that description had been seen with a group of 'suspicious' motorcyclists. Not only did the car have a possible connection to Robles' murder, but the cyclists were definitely instigating trouble in The Sisters.

With his calls made, he turned his attention to his whiteboard and the notes scribbled there.

Victims:
River Co. black male deputy - clubbed over head
Sisters white female medic - shot in leg with 223 rifle
Riverton Hispanic male firefighter - shot to death with undetermined gun
Riverton white male deputy - hit and run (may or may not be connected)
All fire depts. - deliberate fire in field
Sisters VFD - small explosive
Cougar Springs/ River Co. - shots fired into county deputy's home
Riverton Security Guard - injected with unidentified drugs
Sisters PD - poisoned brownies

The incidents had taken place all over the county, specifically in Riverton and The Sisters, but the smaller towns of Cougar Springs and Indian Meadows hadn't been left unscathed.

With a big question mark beside it, Brash added a new entry.

? Community of Low Crossing - robbery - any connection?

Sadly, the list of suspects was significantly smaller.

Only one entry, in fact, held a possible clue—*Motorcycle gang*—and even that was pure conjuncture. There was no clear correlation between any of the crimes, nor between the crimes and the motorcycles.

Completely frustrated, Brash knew they were as clueless today as they had been when this first started.

They *had* to be missing something.

19

By morning, the sheriff's department was no closer to finding the suspects nor their car than they had been the evening before.

The motorcycles, however, had been sighted in Indian Meadows. Constable Lewallen called Brash with the update, warning that the men were seen leaving town and heading toward The Sisters.

"Perry, come with me," Brash barked as he marched from his office. "The motorcycles were sighted and headed this way."

"Need backup?" Schmanski asked.

"No, you stay here and respond to calls. Remember, no solo acts. Abraham is on call with the fire department but can ride with you if she's available."

Even though Nate was out of the hospital, he hadn't been cleared for duty. The best he could do was man a desk. Brash insisted he was being instrumental in another way, scouring through reports of similar attacks on officers in other towns. He was looking for any thread that tied those crimes to their own.

Buckling his seatbelt in Brash's SUV, Otis Perry asked, "What's the plan?"

"We'll take a look out by the highway. If we see

them, we'll follow at a leisurely pace. I want them to know we have our eyes on them. If the Camaro happens to be with them, we'll use lights and sirens and pull it over."

"And if we don't see them? They could take one of the county roads and not come directly into town. They may have somewhere they're staying to lie low."

"We don't have time to chase down people without hard evidence. We don't know they were involved in the robbery, any more than we know they're behind the attacks."

"You didn't see these guys, Brash. They were mean, through and through. I wouldn't put anything past them."

They drove over halfway to Indian Meadows, but the group was nowhere in sight. Brash was turning around to return to the station when the radio went off.

"Cougar Springs to SO. We have an officer down. Repeat! Officer down. Unknown assailant. Send an ambulance and a backup unit."

Brash's knuckles tightened on the wheel and his foot pressed harder on the gas pedal as he told Perry, "Tell them we're fifteen minutes out if they need us."

Cougar Springs had only two officers, and now one was down. The sheriff's department asked Brash to assist. DPS and a sheriff's deputy would be en route, but The Sisters' unit could reach them first.

By the time they arrived, the ambulance was there and loading the deputy into the box. The investigator in Brash took over, and he hit the ground running. "What happened?"

"I-I don't know," a pasty-faced deputy answered from the gurney. His voice sounded scratchy. "I stopped for coffee and was walking back to my car. Something came out of the blue, latched onto my ankle, and jerked me to the ground. I—"

"Sorry," the medic interrupted, "but his chief will have to answer the rest of your questions. He has a concussion and is on blood thinner, so there's a chance of a brain bleed. We need to get him to the hospital."

"Right. Godspeed." Brash stepped away from the ambulance to where Otis Perry was talking to Chief Perkins.

"Hey. Listen to this, boss," Perry said.

The other chief started over. "Marty was about to get into his car when someone roped his feet."

"Did you say *roped*?"

"Sure did. Jerked him down like a calf. Another lasso around his neck pulled him a good five feet and almost choked him to death."

Brash looked around the parking lot of the convenience store, noting the absence of vehicles. "Did anyone see anything?"

"Nope. At this time of day, the morning crowd has already come and gone. Just a few stragglers here and there, and you can see it's not many."

"He was parked over there?" Brash asked, pointing toward the marked car at the far side of the lot.

"Yep. Guess he was leaving plenty of room for customers, but it offered the perfect opportunity for his assailants. The driver's door is facing those trees, so even if it was crowded, no one could see a thing."

"The ropes? Were they still on him?"

"Nope. His assailants pulled a burlap bag over his face, untied the ropes, and were gone before he came to enough to react."

"Which way did they go?"

"Don't know. The cashier doesn't remember seeing a vehicle but can't be sure. For all we know, someone pulled up to the curb, and they hopped in."

"You said assailants, plural. You think there were two?"

"I do." Waylon Perkins nodded. "Sort of like team roping."

"Did he actually lose consciousness?"

"He doesn't think so. He just said he was knocked silly, and for a minute there, he couldn't think of anything but the pain. He had a good wallop to the head, not to mention his back."

"Have you interviewed the cashier? Anyone who may have been at the pumps or inside at the time?"

"There was one woman at the pumps, but she says she didn't see a thing. She was on the phone while pumping gas and not paying attention. The attendant didn't see anything, either."

"Does anyone remember seeing or hearing motorcycles?" Brash asked.

"No one mentioned it if they did."

"Otis, go talk to the attendant. Ask him about the bikes."

Brash walked around the patrol car to where the deputy had gone down. The concrete parking lot made it impossible to see footprints. All he saw was a smear of blood and faint drag marks, most likely made by the deputy's service weapon.

"Given this is ranch country, I imagine there are plenty of good ropers. Any of them team rope in rodeo?" Brash asked.

Perkins rubbed a hand over his whiskered face. The grueling schedule had taken a toll on the man, and he looked as if he hadn't shaved in days. Brash had to wonder if he had even slept. With just two officers on the force, Perkins' days had to be long.

"There's the Monroe twins," he said thoughtfully, "but one of them—I can never tell them apart—broke his arm and is still wearing a cast. The only other team I can think of offhand is Ruby Murchinson and Loreen Hoss."

"This thing keeps getting bigger and bigger, Waylon. There has to be something we're all missing."

"Do you think the biker gang are the ones attacking first responders?"

"It's come up once or twice in conversation. Aside from being at that gas station the night before Robles was killed, Detective Perry had a brief run-in with them when they were harassing my daughter. Still, I think it's too soon to accuse them of staging these attacks. They're bad news, all right, but not necessarily the people we're after."

Perry returned from the store. "The cashier says he didn't see or hear any motorcycles, so I guess that theory's out."

"'What about those businesses over there?" Brash asked Sheriff Perkins, hitching a thumb over his shoulder to indicate a handful of stores across the road. "Would you like us to talk with them and see if anyone saw anything?"

"If you don't mind, yeah. As soon as someone from the sheriff's office gets here, I'd like to go to the hospital and be there for Marty. I've already called his ex-wife, but who knows if she'll show up. They had a rough marriage and an even rougher divorce."

"Absolutely. Go be with your deputy. We have it covered."

"Are you sure?"

"Yeah. Go on," Brash encouraged him. "We'll stay until the SO gets here. Longer, if necessary."

"I know you've got your own troubles over in The Sisters, so I really appreciate this, Brash. You too, deputy." He shook both men's hands before hurrying to his patrol car.

Brash turned to his deputy. "Start on the far right with the beauty shop while I update SO. I'll take the hardware store on the left. We'll meet up somewhere in the middle."

The interviews didn't net any results. By that time, the sheriff's office had arrived, and Brash gladly left them in charge. There was a fender bender in Naomi, so that meant they were shorthanded at the station, and he was anxious to get back.

Plus, there was always the motorcycle gang to consider. According to Wanda Shanks, they had been in town two nights ago, and there was a likely chance they would return.

It was a long day, and Otis caught the brunt of it. Brash was tied up in a meeting with Sheriff Larson and a liaison with the US Marshals Service Larson had called in to assist. With crimes taking place all over the county and each department stretched thin, they needed all the help they could get.

With a rival football team in town for the Friday night ballgame, Otis would be back on duty at the high school stadium. Brash insisted he leave for a bit, at least long enough to eat and take a breather.

Otis chose a quiet booth at *Montelongo's* to enjoy his downtime. The last two weeks had been non-stop, and his old body was feeling it. It crossed his mind that he should give some serious thought to retirement. The thought was fleeting, replaced by the knowledge that he had little life outside the department.

Halfway through his meal, he felt the presence of someone beside his table. He looked up to see what some people called the Terrible Threesome: Sybil, Wanda, and Bertha. In his mind, the term would be more accurate if Virgie Adams replaced Sybil. When *that* woman and Bertha Cessna teamed up, trouble wasn't far behind. With her husband Hank ailing lately, Virgie hadn't been running with her friends as much, but word had it that Hank was on the mend. Soon enough, she would be back in the thick of things, and then he might reconsider his retirement.

"Hello, Deputy," Sybil said politely.

Behind her, Granny Bert managed a stiff murmur of a greeting. Wanda was so tipsy after two margaritas that she only giggled.

"Evening, ladies." He kept his eyes on Sybil, snubbing her companions. Clearly, he didn't include them in the term.

"I hope you enjoyed the refreshments I left for you."

"I always enjoy your fine cooking, Sybil."

Pleased with his compliment, she nodded toward his unfinished meal. "We'll let you get on with your supper. We just wanted to stop by and say hello."

As the women departed, Otis heard Granny Bert snort. "There was no 'we' to it! Are you still apologizing to that old coot for what happened at Wanda's?"

Hearing her name, Wanda asked, "What happened at Wanda's?"

Sidestepping the remark about Otis, Sybil remarked, "It's a good thing you're driving her home. No telling where she might wind up if she was behind the wheel."

"The ditch, most likely," Granny Bert grumbled.

As he polished off his enchiladas, Otis thought of how good a slice of Sybil's buttermilk pie or one of her brownies would taste for dessert. He'd have to settle for a packaged honey bun or apple fritter on his way to the ballgame.

The convenience store out on the highway was a bit out of the way, but they carried the brand he preferred. He made the short trip and was heading back to his patrol car when he heard a familiar voice behind him.

"Well, look what the cat dragged up," the man said in a slow drawl. "Course, it would have to be a mighty big cat to drag that sort of weight."

Otis turned around slowly, knowing he would see one or more bikers behind him.

He was relieved to see there was only one. Unfortunately, he was also the biggest of the lot: the black man with the bald head and the bulging biceps.

Otis mustered as much attitude as he could manage. "Come to hit this store, too, did you?"

The big man's eyes narrowed. "What do you mean, 'too?'"

"Exactly what I said. Maybe you weren't the one to pull it off, but you knew what your buddies were doing. That makes you an accessory to a crime."

"What crime, pig? I don't know what you're talking about."

"I'm talking about a robbery at a small engine repair shop in Low Crossing last night, right at closing time. The owner was settling up the till when your two buddies knocked him over the head and relieved him of the cash."

"What makes you think they were my buddies?"

Otis shrugged, somehow looking cavalier about the whole conversation. In truth, his knees threatened to give way, but he couldn't let the other man know that. "They fit the description of your running buddies."

"Coulda been anybody," he claimed.

"Driving the same blue souped-up Camaro seen with you and your gang? I doubt it."

"I ain't their babysitter, pig. What they do on their own time don't concern me none."

"Just when you're carrying out gang activities, huh?"

"Hey! Unless you want us to *gang* up on your fat butt, I'd keep my trap shut if I was you."

"Is that a threat?"

"Take it how you like it. Just know that I got my eye on you. Watch your step," he threatened.

Without another word, the big man straddled his motorcycle and kicked it in gear. As he rode off in the night, he flipped off the deputy watching his departure.

A chill stole over Otis Perry, and it had nothing to do with the pleasant fall weather.

20

Saturday was Madison's last day to work at *Tammy's Treasure*, and she was certain she would miss the little shop. She not only enjoyed the merchandise, but she enjoyed the interaction with Tammy's customers. She thought the store owner was fortunate to have such a popular business next door. *Miss Zuri's* was twice as active as the gift shop, but it provided a trickle-over effect that kept the door fanning at Tammy's.

When she wasn't busy with her own customers, Madison had enjoyed people-watching Miss Zuri's. The buildings along this side of the street still sported the old style, with brick facades, display windows out front, and recessed entrances shared with the business next door. In just the few days she had been there, Madison had watched as people from all walks of life stepped onto the sidewalk and disappeared through her doors.

The talented masseuse had a wide range of clientele. Her customers included teenagers, old women like her grandmother's friends, middle-aged women such as herself, and a handful of men. They seemed to come from all walks of life. Girls in their cheerleader uniforms. Athletes in their workout gear. A pair of middle-aged women in their fancy western attire, most likely wearing Sticker Pierce boots. Men in casual attire, and one in suit and tie. There was no clear pattern to the clients pouring in next door; everyone seemed to love Miss Zuri.

Granny Bert was one of Madison's last customers of the day. She said she was there to offer moral support, but Madison saw the look on her grandmother's face. Something was bothering her.

After Granny Bert roamed the store and only brought a greeting card back to the register, Madison gave her a speculative look. "Okay. What it is? Are you and Miss Sybil on the outs again?"

Her grandmother didn't pretend ignorance. "Not yet," she sniffed. "But we're fixin' to be."

"Why is that?"

"You know how I told you I thought Sybil was seeing someone?"

"Sure. And I agree."

"And remember how I said there no reason for her to hide it from me, because the only man I would object to her seeing was Otis Perry?"

"Yes. And I agree with you there, too."

"Well, I think we both need to object."

Madison didn't understand at first, but when the words finally sank in, her eyes went wide. Even with both hands over her mouth, she couldn't hold in a gasp.

"You can't be serious!"

"I'm not one hundred percent certain, but it's a weak one percent that's holding out."

"Whatever makes you think she's seeing Otis Perry? And whatever is *she* thinking, getting involved with him?"

"Obviously, she's not thinking. She knows the history between Otis and me. Even though we've mended a few of our fences, there's still a whole section down, and I'm thinking more is about to tumble."

"What brought you to this conclusion? Why Otis?"

"It's been a lot of things. You even told me how strangely he reacted to her attacking him with scissors. You said he was oddly tender with her. If I had done that, he would have come after me with all he had. And the way he showed up at her house later that evening, and her wanting me to go. Then, last night, we saw him at *Montelongo's* last night, and Sybil insisted we stop and say hello. There was something about the way they were looking at each other... And then she mentioned something about the refreshments she left for him. He said he always appreciated her fine cooking, and I swear she blushed like a smitten schoolgirl with her first crush." Granny Bert crossed her arms over her chest and huffed out a long, disgruntled breath. "I'm telling you; she's defected and gone over to the other side. An eighty-year friendship down the drain, just like that!"

"Now, Granny," Madison tried reasoning with her. "Even if she is seeing Otis—and let's give her the benefit of the doubt until we know for sure—that's no reason to turn your back on your oldest and dearest friend."

"If she is seeing him, then she turned her back on me. It amounts to treason!"

"Granny, think about what you're saying. Neither of us are fans of Otis Perry, but if Miss Sybil finds happiness at this point in her life, who are we to judge? If he makes her happy, we should be sharing her happiness."

"Not going to happen," her grandmother said stubbornly. "The man is ten years younger than her, and a hundred pounds heavier. They have nothing in common, other than she likes to cook, and he likes to eat."

"He may be fifty pounds heavier," Madison allowed,

"but a hundred is pushing it. And I'm sure there are other things they have in common."

"I can't think of a one."

"What if Miss Sybil had done that to you and Sticker? He's younger than you and shorter, too. He's a rodeo legend and cowboy to the core. You're a public servant and don't even like horses. What do you have in common?"

"History. We have history together." Granny Bert shook her finger in Madison's face to make her point. "You know he was my first love, long before I fell for your grandfather. For as long as I can remember, Sybil's had almost as much against Otis as I have. You can't make a one-eighty like that and expect everyone to understand, much less to be happy about it!"

"But you owe it to Miss Sybil—and to your friendship—to at least try to accept her relationship with him."

"I don't know about that," her grandmother grumbled.

"Talk to her, Granny," Madison urged. "Hear what she has to say. You may be wrong about the whole situation. But if you're not, you need to hear her out and try to understand her feelings."

After a moment of pure stubbornness, Granny Bert finally budged. "I guess it wouldn't hurt to hear what she has to say."

"Of course not! And it will make you feel better, knowing you gave her the benefit of the doubt and remained a tried-and-true friend."

"I already agreed to do it," her grandmother continued to grumble. "Don't overdo it on the flowery speech."

"Yes, ma'am," Madison murmured demurely, trying to hide a smile.

Yet after she had gone, Madison shook her head and

muttered, "Miss Sybil and Otis Perry? What is this world coming to? I thought she had better sense than to get involved with *him!*"

Between her job at *Tammy's* coming to an end and the mere thought of The Sisters' latest couple, Madison felt oddly depressed. A last-minute shopping spree on her part lifted her spirits. She had been eying a few things she was certain the girls would love, and it was never too soon to start Christmas shopping. She even found a cute top she liked. Derron was always encouraging her to try something other than her tried-and-true classic style, and this was something new and different.

Madison wore a smile as she locked the shop one last time. After just three days there, she knew she would return many times as a customer. Several boxes had been delivered the day before, and she was anxious to see the new inventory. Tammy had an eye for unique treasures.

Stepping off the sidewalk, Madison had no idea of what the rest of the day held in store. What happened next would rock the very foundation of her world.

The call came at dusk.

"SO to Sisters PD. We have reports of suspicious activity at and around 212 Meadows. The caller sounds upset and would like someone to check it out."

Brash and Otis were at the coffee pot, pouring a cup of liquid energy after a particularly busy day. Otis was on duty for the night, and it was Brash's turn as backup for the fire department. With a ton of paperwork yet to do, he opted to make use of his on-call status.

Hearing the call, Otis spat out a mouthful of coffee. Before Brash could complain, the older man cried, "That's Sybil's house!"

Brash grabbed his radio. "SO, this is Chief deCordova. What else did the caller say?"

"Sisters PD, she reported several motorcycles driving up and down the streets, and now she hears sounds coming from her backyard. She's worried, afraid someone is out there."

"10-4, SO. Show us en route."

Otis was already halfway to the door. "Motorcycles! I knew those men were nothing but trouble!"

"Take a minute, Otis, and calm down," Brash advised as he settled his cowboy hat atop his head. "We don't know that they've done anything."

"Except scare poor Sybil half out of her mind!"

Curious about the unprecedented worry in his deputy's voice, Brash followed him out to the cruiser. Otis crawled behind the wheel and took off before Brash's door clicked shut.

"Slow down, Otis!" Brash demanded. "We can't help Miss Sybil if we don't make it there in one piece."

Otis slowed the car marginally, which Brash suspected took great restraint. He watched Otis run a hand over the back of his bald head and blow out a steadying breath.

"Is there anything you want to tell me, Otis?"

Without looking at him—a good thing, since they were still driving at an unsafe speed—Otis was evasive. "I don't know what you mean."

"Of course you do," Brash challenged.

Another deep exhale. Otis finally answered as he turned a corner too sharply and jostled them both. "Fine. Sybil and I have been quiet about it, but we've been seeing each other for about a month now."

Brash managed not to sound as shocked as he felt. "Really." It was more a statement than question.

"She's a wonderful woman, Brash."

"You don't have to convince me of that. Maddy and

I are both very fond of Miss Sybil."

"I swear, if those motorcycle thugs have laid one hand on her..." He tightened his hand on the steering wheel until his knuckles turned white.

"She reported hearing and seeing something suspicious, Otis, not someone breaking down her door. Just get us there safely and we'll assess the situation."

Two more potholes, another screeching corner, and they reached the neatly maintained home just outside of town. Brash put a hand on Otis' arm to keep him from jumping out of the car.

"Hold on. We need to do a visual. Make sure this isn't a set-up."

"Do you hear yourself? This is *Sybil* we're talking about!"

"I didn't say *she* was setting us up. I'm saying she reported seeing the bikers, but they aren't here now. How do we know they haven't staged an ambush?"

"You have a point, but she doesn't know it's us out here. She's probably more scared than ever," Otis worried.

"Then call her, tell her it's us, and that we'll check things out before speaking with her."

Brash concentrated on the multiplying shadows as Otis made his call. He was looking for any tell-tale signs of movement along the edges of the house or something metallic reflecting in the weak light. As he studied the growing darkness, he thought he saw something. Was that a person off to the left or a misshaped tree? The hairs on the back of his neck stood at attention. Something about this felt off.

"You ready?" he asked his deputy. "Stay alert. I've got a bad feeling about this one."

"Do we split up or go together?"

"Together. We need to have each other's back." They exited the car and cautiously moved forward.

Brash motioned to the left, indicating they would start that way.

It was the time of day when time seemed suspended between daylight and dark. That time when images were distorted, and edges were fuzzy. Too late for sunlight, too early for moonlight. The time of day when it was hard to see, and when a person questioned the reliability of their eyes.

As they approached the left side of the house, Brash gave a cursory look at the path ahead, making certain no obstacles littered the way. Rosebushes, bird feeders, and various planters were scattered throughout the yard, but once they passed the wisteria tree, the pathway was clear.

Turning his attention back to the shadowy outlines to his left, Brash never saw the trip wire. It caught his booted foot and sent him sprawling, chest down, as his gun flew out of his hand.

Otis' reflexes were slow, but he managed not to make the same mistake. "What the—" The rest of his words were swallowed in a yelp of pain. Something sharp stuck his shoulder, as pain raced a trail down his pudgy arm. There was enough light for him to look down and see an arrow protruding from his flesh. A wave of nausea mingled with disbelief, and he instantly knew they were in trouble.

"Brash?"

Around a groan of pain, Brash warned, "Get down, Perry!"

"I—I can't. I've been hit. An arrow."

"Then take cover!"

"Where?" Otis' voice was frantic. It was growing darker, but he could see well enough to know there was nothing to hide behind.

"The wisteria," Brash hissed. He scrambled up on all fours, across the wire, and reached Otis. The man was already swaying on his feet.

"Crouch down, Otis, and get over to that tree!" Brash tugged on his hand, pulling Otis down and along. The tree was little more than an overgrown plant, but it was all they had.

He put himself between his deputy and the unknown shooter. His mind raced, recalling that the grass fire had been started by a flaming arrow. Was a member of the motorcycle club prolific in archery, or was this someone else entirely? He made a mental note to check out all archery shops in the surrounding areas.

Brash suspected that, at a minimum, his collarbone was broken in the fall, but it didn't stop him. He tugged a stumbling Otis along with one hand, while with the other, he pressed his radio's call button.

"Sisters PD to SO. Officer down! Arrow wound to his left shoulder. Unknown assailant. Send ambulance and back up to 212 Meadows. Repeat, send—*oomph!*" Brash's loud grunt of pain cut his transmission short.

He felt the arrow rip through his flesh, burying itself deep into his right side. Pain exploded in his abdomen, and the air escaped from his lungs. Blood was already soaking his shirt. He felt himself falling, knowing he would inevitably drag Otis down with him. He tugged his deputy to the right, hoping Otis wouldn't fall on the arrow protruding from his left shoulder. Brash twisted his own body left, trying to protect his injured right side from the crash landing.

He never even felt the second arrow as it struck him in the thigh.

By then, Brash was succumbing to mind-numbing pain and the heavy loss of blood.

Everything went black.

21

Madison raced through the sliding doors of the emergency department, frantically looking for the front desk. She spied a glass-fronted cubicle on the left. A man stood in front of the window, producing his medical insurance card.

Practically pushing him aside, Madison panted, "My husband! My husband's in there! I need to see him!"

"Ma'am! Wait your turn!" admonished the receptionist.

"I can't! My husband is a police officer. He's been shot! They told me to hurry!"

"I'm afraid you'll have to wait your turn, ma'am, or I'll be forced to call security."

There was a sound of booted feet behind her, and someone called her name. "Maddy!" Plain-clothes College Station Detective Cade Resnick was suddenly at her side. Taking her arm, he gave the receptionist a commanding look. "That won't be necessary. She's with me. Open the doors. We'll take the ER staff elevator up."

"You can't do that! It's for hospital personnel only."

"Are you trying to obstruct justice?" Cade asked,

flashing his badge.

"N-no, sir. Of course not, sir," the woman stammered.

"Head Nurse Laurel Benson is waiting for us. And see that anyone with Mrs. deCordova is escorted to the surgery waiting room immediately."

A gasp strangled Madison's throat. "Surgery?"

"I'll explain on the way up." Guiding Madison toward the ER unit, he looked back at the receptionist. "The doors?"

"Yes. Of course." She pressed the button to swing the heavy doors open.

"What happened, Cade? Why is Brash in surgery? Vina didn't know any details. She just said to hurry!"

"I see Laurel up ahead. She can explain it better than I can."

After enveloping her friend in a hug, Laurel whisked them all into the elevator and up to the second floor. Without preamble, Laurel explained, "Brash was shot with two arrows. The—"

"*Arrows*? As in bow and arrow?" Madison tried to make sense of what she was hearing, but at that moment, nothing made sense. Brash was hurt and in surgery! Where was the sense in that?

"Yes. He and a deputy were responding to a call when they came under attack. The deputy was hit in the shoulder and the way I understand it, Brash was trying to protect him. He put himself between the deputy and the shooter, and in the process, he was hit by additional arrows. One hit him in the side, the other in his thigh."

"How is he? Why is he in surgery? Is he going to be all right?"

The elevator binged as it delivered them to the surgical floor. Mingled with fear and worry, the strong astringent smell made Madison feel lightheaded.

"We'll go to one of the waiting rooms," Laurel

murmured, leading the way down a corridor.

The moment she opened the door to a softly lit room with two sofas and several comfy chairs, Madison knew this was a private waiting room. A room she didn't want to be in because it was reserved for families waiting to hear the very worst. The night she learned that Gray hadn't survived the car crash, she had been led to a similar room in a different hospital. *Did they all look like this?* she wondered idly. She was experiencing a strange sense of déjà vu.

"Tell me, Laurel." She put her hand on the nurse's arm. Her voice came out deadly calm. "Tell me the truth."

"He's in critical condition, Maddy, but he's strong, and he's stubborn. He was unconscious when the ambulance arrived."

The door opened to the waiting room and in rushed the family. Megan, Brash's parents, Granny Bert, and Genny all crowded through the door. The room was large enough to accommodate everyone, but Cade quietly stepped out.

"How's Daddy?" Megan demanded. The question ran together with, "Trenton is driving Bethani here from Huntsville, and Blake is on his way from Waco."

"Laura is coming, too, and maybe Joshua," Andrew said, referring to Brash's sister and one of his brothers.

"How's my son?" Lydia wanted to know, still holding her daughter-in-law in a hug.

"Laurel was about to tell me." With a weak smile, Madison expounded, "Brash was being his usual noble self, protecting one of his deputies. They were both shot by arrows."

Her father-in-law's forehead crinkled with a frown. "Did you say—"

"Yes, an arrow. Laurel, could you start over?"

"Certainly." She waited for everyone to settle into a

seat. Andrew remained standing.

"Brash was hit in the side with the first arrow," Laurel explained, "and in the thigh with the second. He lost consciousness at the scene but was somewhat alert when they took him in for surgery."

"Why surgery?" Andrew demanded. "How much damage was done?"

Laurel took a deep breath before giving an honest answer. "The doctors will know more once they get in there but for starters, he has one punctured lung, a chipped rib, damage to his gallbladder and possibly the liver, plus extensive muscle damage to his abdomen and his right thigh."

"For starters!" Megan cried out. "Isn't that enough?"

"We'll know more when the doctor comes out," Laurel repeated, touching her hand.

"What are his chances, Laurel?" Never one to mince her words, Granny Bert asked the question on everyone's mind.

"I won't sugarcoat it. Brash is in critical condition. He's bleeding internally, and that's one of the main reasons for surgery. If they can find the source and stop it, his chances should go up drastically."

"And if they don't?" Lydia dared ask.

"The doctor can tell you more. I'm a trauma nurse, but I'm no surgeon." She stood and motioned for Andrew to take her place. "I'll let you have a little time to yourself. There's coffee and refreshments in the main waiting room, just through the double doors. You'll need to use the keypad to get back in. The code is 9797. I'll be back in if I have any news." She paused beside the door. "It could be a long night, so settle in and make yourselves comfortable. There are fresh blankets in the cabinet beneath the television. Help yourselves."

"Thank you, Laurel," Genny spoke for them all.

"Of course. You have my cell if you need me."

Megan wiggled her way between Grammy and Mama Maddy, needing the comfort of both. These were the three women who loved Brash the most, and they needed to be there for him, and for each other.

"He's going to be okay, Megan," Madison said, holding her stepdaughter's hand.

"You know how stubborn your father can be," Lydia added, hugging her granddaughter against her side. "He'll fight and claw his way back to full health. He's like his own father in that regard. Too ornery to ever give up," she said, flashing her eyes toward her husband.

"She's right," Andrew seconded. "We deCordova men don't give up. We're made of stronger stuff than some little arrow. And you are, too, girl. Don't forget that."

"I'm scared," Megan admitted, sounding like a little girl again.

"So am I, sweetie," Madison told her, "but we can't let your father know that. When he comes out of surgery—and he will, don't you doubt that for one minute! —he needs to see our smiling faces. Think you can do that for him?"

Megan nodded, practicing a smile through her tears.

"I didn't even think to ask," Madison realized after a while. "What other officer was shot?"

"Otis Perry." Granny Bert's mouth turned downward. "Brash risked his life for Otis Perry."

"Does it surprise you?" Madison asked softly. "He risks his life every day, for people he doesn't even know."

"How is Berry Perry?" Genny asked, using the nickname from the past. It wasn't one derived from affection.

"Lost a good bit of blood, but the arrow didn't hit anything major. Knowing him, he'll be back out on the streets soon enough, complaining about young people in general and me and Virgie, in particular."

"Don't forget me. He's had a grudge against me since I was in high school," Genny said. "And I suspect he only tolerates Maddy because she's married to his boss."

More of the family trickled in. Bethani and her boyfriend arrived first, followed by Brash's siblings. Vina was next. She was family, too. Blake was the last to arrive. Madison comforted her son, knowing how close he was to Brash. He had bonded with him in a way he had never bonded with Gray, which humbled Brash and made Maddy proud.

With each retelling of what damage the arrows had done, something nibbled at the edges of Madison's mind. She knew there was something she was missing, but she couldn't quite remember what. Her mind was numb with worry. As the clock ticked away the evening and worked its way to midnight, fatigue set in. Laurel had been right. It would be a long night.

When Shannon and her husband arrived and the facts were repeated, Madison felt it again, that little nudge telling her to think harder. Brash had mentioned arrows before, hadn't he? She would ask Vina. Vina knew everything that happened at the police station and then some.

She looked around and didn't find Brash's most trusted colleague. She remembered then that Vina and some of the others had moved to the main waiting room as more and more bodies crowded into the smaller space. As the number of Brash's supporters grew, the generous size of the room seemed to shrink.

When Laurel's shift ended, she came back in to

check on them. The only real news she had was they had removed Brash's gall bladder, and that the damage to his thigh wasn't as extensive as originally feared. A nurse from the surgical unit had given two other updates throughout the evening, but none were the news his family wanted to hear: that he was out of danger and would make a full recovery.

After six grueling hours, the doctor finally came out. He looked as exhausted as the rest of them.

"The good news is that we stopped the internal bleeding." He launched into a simplified version of long medical terms and explanations, but Madison concentrated on his leading point. *Good news.*

For the first time since she got the call, she could fully breathe.

"The bad news?" Andrew asked, sensing there was more.

"He's still not out of danger. That arrow did a lot of damage, and we think that the broad head may have been laced with something. There's an extraordinary amount of inflammation and unhealthy cells surrounding the wound, suggesting a foreign agent. Until we can identify the source and start the appropriate antibiotic or treatment, he's at an increased danger of infection. There's the matter of his punctured lung and the possibility that pneumonia could set in. Frankly, at this point, there are a number of things that could go wrong, but the upside is that he's in excellent physical condition, he's strong, and he's healthy. Those are all positives that weigh heavily in his favor."

"What kind of foreign agent?" Blake asked.

"We're not sure yet."

"I think I know," Madison said.

The doctor looked surprised. "You do?"

"Someone has been targeting first responders in

our area. Earlier this week, one of Brash's deputies ingested poison that had been slipped into a batch of brownies left at the police department. He was treated here at Texas General. My guess is that the attacker used the same or similar poison to soak the broad heads."

"I'll definitely look into that. What was the deputy's name?"

"Nate Stone. He was released on... Wednesday?" She looked at Megan for confirmation.

"Yes, that's right. The ambulance brought him in the day before."

"That's good to know. Thank you, ladies," the doctor said. He surveyed the small crowd around them. "I know everyone wants to be here, but there's really nothing you can do. The next twelve to eighteen hours will tell us more about his condition and what comes next. This won't be a fast recovery, so you need to pace yourselves. There will be plenty of time to sit with him in the days to come. My advice is to go home, get some sleep, have a bite to eat, and reconvene tomorrow. We'll have a better picture of his condition at that time."

Madison knew most of them wouldn't leave, but she thanked the doctor for all he had done to save Brash's life.

"There's more family in the general waiting room," she added. "Could you go with me to update them and tell them the same thing about going home to get some rest?"

"Of course." He glanced around the room at the weary faces and slumped shoulders. "And I strongly urge all of you to take my advice. Get some sleep."

Out in the hallway, the doctor handed Madison a business card with the words Courtesy Card written across the top. "Show this to the receptionist in the ICU waiting room. It's a concierge suite we reserve for the family of select patients. Dignitaries and such," he explained.

Madison was touched. "That's very generous of you."

"It's the least we can do. Law officers don't get the respect and recognition they deserve. In my eyes, your husband is just as important, if not more so, than the politicians and celebrities and foreign dignitaries the room was created for. He was hurt in the line of duty, and we all owe a huge debt to men like your husband. And to the families who stand behind them and support them every day."

"It's the weight of the badge," Madison murmured.

Perhaps for the first time, the magnitude of that weight pressed into her heart and stifled her breath.

Brash remained in post-op for the remainder of the night. As the waiting room cleared out, Maddy, their three children, his parents, and Granny Bert remained. Grabbing blankets and a seat, they settled in for a long and restless night.

As a new day broke, a nurse came out to say Brash was being moved to the ICU. She warned it would be a while before anyone could see him but suggested they move to the waiting room there.

Once they arrived in their new location, Madison showed the courtesy card the doctor had given her, and they were led to a posh suite. It had leather furnishings, its own refreshment bar, and a private restroom.

"Wow. I didn't know there was anything like this in College Station. This is fancy," Bethani said, sinking into a sofa.

"The college has a lot of important people coming through their doors. Leaders of the state, foreign diplomats, a celebrity or two... I guess everyone gets sick or injured at some point," her mother reasoned.

"It doesn't hurt that a former president considered this area his home," Blake added. "The George H. Bush Presidential Library is here. That brings in a lot of big wigs. They expect this level of comfort."

"As far as I'm concerned, our father *is* a celebrity," Megan said. "Even if we don't deserve all this, he does."

"On that note, I think I'll try out that fancy coffee machine," Madison said. "I may have slept through my last hourly dose."

"You're going to be so wired, you won't sleep for a week," Bethani predicted.

"Once I know your father's going to be all right, *then* I'll sleep."

22

Madison and Megan were the first to go in. Brash's face was pale and drawn against the white sheets. Tubes and wires were attached in random places. It broke Madison's heart to see her strong husband in such a vulnerable state. She knew he would hate it, being exposed and helpless like this.

Unsure whether he could hear them, they spoke in uplifting voices, talking about all the things they would do once he was out of the hospital. Madison wished she could stay longer, but she knew the others wanted to see him. They all *needed* to see him, to assure themselves that he had made it through surgery and was still fighting.

Before leaving, she leaned close to kiss him and whisper in his ear, "I love you so much, Brash. And I swear, I will do everything in my power to help find the people who did this to you." Sniffing back tears, she caressed his handsome face. "I love you, sweetheart, and I need you back home with me. We can fight this. I know we can."

She and Megan leaned into one another as they left the room. Once in the corridor, their tears freely flowed. They had kept it together for Brash's sake, but they fell apart now.

"He looked so helpless!" Megan sobbed. "I've never seen him like that. He's always been so strong. So indestructible."

"He still is," Madison insisted fiercely. "He'll fight this by sheer will."

Megan nodded, managing a smile. "When he sets his mind on something, he's as stubborn as a mule."

"Isn't that the truth?" Tugging her along, Madison said, "We don't need to let the others see us crying. They'll think the worst. We need to dry our tears and put on a brave face."

With that in mind, they stepped into the concierge suite wearing what they hoped were optimistic expressions.

The rules allowed only two visitors at a time, so when Granny Bert waited to take the last turn, Madison went in again with her.

More family and friends showed up throughout the day but to Madison, the hours and the faces blurred. Brash was no better now than he was when he went into ICU, and she was worried sick. She couldn't eat, couldn't sleep, and couldn't concentrate.

The day dragged into night. Night dragged into another new dawn. Still, she refused to leave.

By the end of the second day, there was finally some good news. Having identified the poison used to saturate the broad heads, the new treatment plan was working. The doctors cautiously upgraded his status from critical to serious. It was an improvement, no matter how slight.

On the third day, Lydia insisted that Madison get out for a while. The girls had brought her fresh clothes, but she was unable to bathe or wash her hair. When Laurel offered her house yet again, Madison took her up on the offer. A long, soaking bath in the old claw-foot tub was exactly what she needed.

Feeling almost like a new woman, Madison fixed her hair and makeup, put on her new blouse from *Tammy's*, and headed back to the hospital.

"Hey, there," Genny greeted her when she arrived.

"Genny! Cutter! I didn't know you were here. Why didn't you call me?" she asked as she hugged them both.

"We knew you needed the break. And it looks like it did you good. I finally see some color in those cheeks," Genny said.

"It's a wonder what a hot, soaking bath can do."

"Imagine what a few hours sleeping in a comfy bed would feel like," Lydia chided. "You really should have stayed and taken a nap."

"I'm doing fine on this sofa here." Madison took a seat on said sofa before noticing the crease in Cutter's forehead. He wasn't exactly frowning. She suspected worry had carved a groove there, much as it had done to her own.

"What's wrong, Cutter? Has something more happened?" Her breath caught with a hitch.

"There was another bogus call, this one in Riverton."

Madison closed her eyes briefly, wondering if another family was going through the same misery as them. "Was anyone hurt?"

"A medic," Cutter acknowledged. "The caller said a motorcycle swerved into their path and ran them off the road, but when the fire department and the ambulance arrived, they couldn't find the car. One of the medics walked further down the road to look for fresh skid marks when someone fired at him. Clipped him on the shoulder. Fired a second time and missed."

"No one saw anything?"

"Nothing."

Madison got up to pace the room. "How is this happening, Cutter? How are these people orchestrating all these attacks? Different towns, different targets, different methods. All with no witnesses. This is absolutely crazy!"

"I agree. Sheriff Larson called not only the US Marshals Service but now the Texas Rangers, too. With the police departments all shorthanded and suffering injuries, they've offered to step in and take up some of the slack."

"Who's taking Brash's place?"

"Ranger Barrington. He's one of the best. Almost as good as Brash," Cutter said, lightening the mood with his show-stopping grin.

Genny did her part to change the subject. "Hey, that's a cute top. Is it new?"

"Yes. I bought it from *Tammy's Treasures.*"

"I wonder if she has a similar one in my size." Where Madison was tall and slender, her best friend had more curves and less height.

"I saw a taupe one that would really bring out your blue eyes, and I think it comes in all sizes."

Lydia mentioned a piece of jewelry she had gotten there, and soon they were embroiled in a new conversation.

Madison was only half-listening. Something nibbled at her mind, the way it had the day Brash was shot. She had been too weary to give it another thought since then, but now that she was somewhat refreshed, an uneasy thought wedged itself inside her brain. There was something she needed to remember, but for the life of her, she didn't know what that 'something' was.

By that evening, the doctors were pleased with Brash's progress even though he had yet to wake up. They assured his family that it wasn't uncommon in such circumstances. It was part of the body's self-survival mode, they said. Sometimes, as one doctor put it, that meant 'shutting down the motherboard' and allowing the system to reboot and reset.

Madison encouraged Megan and the twins to return to their classes, even if it meant commuting each day. After checking in on their father, they could go to a hotel for a good night's rest. She had already scouted out family suites available in town.

"I'd love to, Mom," Blake said mournfully, "but I really need to get back to campus. It's part of my scholarship requirements. Believe me, I'd like nothing better than to spend every minute at his bedside, but I promise I'll come every other day. I don't mind sleeping on the couch or in a chair. In fact, I've kind of gotten used to it by now."

"Hopefully, he'll be moved to a private room soon, where there aren't as many restrictions, and we can stay in the room. But there's no need to come every other day, Blake. Just make it when you can."

"But I want to, Mom. He's my dad."

Hearing the way his voice broke brought on a fresh batch of tears. Madison clasped her son in her arms and thanked him for loving Brash so much. She insisted Blake be the first to go in when visiting hours resumed. She allowed him the time alone, knowing there were some things he probably needed to say without an audience.

When Laurel heard Madison was thinking of getting a hotel for the girls, she insisted they stay with her. It was one less worry to deal with.

The next day, with the kids all gone back to classes and their concierge suite empty for a change, the nurses allowed Madison to sit with her husband in his ICU room. She held his hand and rambled softly, talking about anything and everything. She wanted her voice to be the first thing he heard when he awoke.

Around noon, as she launched into yet another tale of Derron's latest antics while she was out of the office, she heard a scratchy sound. It took her a moment to realize it the rusty sound of Brash's voice.

"Maddy?" After four days of silence, his throat was parched, and his voice was hoarse.

"Brash! Brash, you're awake!" she leapt from the chair and gripped the bedrail.

"Do me... a favor," he said in a weak, halting voice.

"Of course! Anything! What do you need me to do, sweetheart?"

He attempted a smile. His words were sluggish. "I need you to... shut up... and kiss me."

With a laugh of pure joy, Maddy obliged him. Then, she was back to talking. "Brash, you had us all so scared! We were worried half out of our minds!"

"Still talking," he complained.

She peppered him with more kisses, mingled with questions of how he felt, did he need the nurse, and if he knew why he was there.

"Got shot. Arrow." He spoke in abbreviated sentences, but he was speaking. That's what was important.

"Yes. And before you ask, Otis is fine. The arrow that hit him was clean. They kept him two nights and released him. Probably because he was too ornery to put up with, but they claimed he could rest just as well at home."

"Catch them?"

She knew he was asking if they had caught the people behind the attacks. "Not yet, but the Rangers are on the case now. A Ranger Barrington is filling in for you."

He mumbled an unintelligible reply before falling back to sleep.

Madison was all smiles as she shot off an email to

the family, sharing the good news with their loved ones.

Only then did she slip out to find a nurse.

After one more day in ICU, Brash was moved to a private room. It granted much more space and a chance for the family to be with him at one time.

As more friends and family came to visit, Madison allowed herself the freedom to get out and stretch her legs. She would walk to the cafeteria, along the corridors, or outside to sit in the sun. A few times, she ventured off the hospital campus, splurging on a drive-through meal or a fancy cup of coffee.

By Saturday, one week after the attack, all three kids were there, as were several other family members. With their encouragement, and at Brash's insistence, she went home for the day. She needed to wash clothes, pack a proper suitcase, and get a few things that Brash requested. Lounge pants and his razor were at the top of his list.

All alone in the house, the rambling old mansion was too quiet. She was eager to return to the hospital, yet she still needed time to unwind. There was nothing quite so exhausting as sitting in a hospital room all day. Doing so for a week was enough to deplete anyone's energy.

On a whim, Madison decided to treat herself to a quick session at *Miss Zuri's*. There was one opening for a massage, and she quickly snapped it up. She could have her car already packed, stop in for the much-needed massage, and be back at the hospital before Brash's dinner tray arrived.

Not surprisingly, *Miss Zuri's Essentials* was busy. Madison waited at the oxygen bar, inhaling a refreshing peppermint scent to revive her spirits. She concentrated on keeping her mind unfocused, trying to tune out the chatter around her.

Maybe the doctor was right about shutting down the brain's computer system. She could do with a reboot about now.

When it was her turn in the massage room, Madison allowed the soft tribal music and the lyrical sound of Miss Zuri's voice to lull her into a deep state of relaxation. Her mind drifted off to an empty space where there were no worries. No fear. Simply nothing.

"Feels good, does it not?" Miss Zuri asked.

"Feels divine."

"You are tight. Worse than before."

"It's been a tough week."

"Yes, I heard. Let Madam Zuri take care of you."

A contented *hmmm* was her reply.

Miss Zuri spoke the strange language again, a singsong of exotic words and foreign intonement. As the music intensified, Madison felt herself frowning.

Was it Miss Zuri, she lazily wondered, *or Madame Zuri?* She felt suddenly confused, but she didn't understand why.

When Miss Zuri hit a particularly sore spot, a bolt of pain jostled Madison from her dream-like state. She tried regaining the bliss of pure relaxation, but the spell had been broken. Her mind came out of its stupor, and her muscles tightened again.

Let it go, Maddy, she told herself. *Relax. Think mundane thoughts. Count sheep.*

Or people. She could count the people she had seen in the spa today.

Hmm. There was the woman with the really red hair. The two women she had seen before, the ones wearing western wear. (Those were *definitely* Sticker Pierce boots.) There was a man she recognized as a 4-H leader; didn't he have a role in some outdoorsy sport like fishing or camping? There was a friend of Granny Bert's from Bunco, and a woman on crutches sitting near the door, who looked as if she were waiting for a ride. *Hmm. Had she forgotten anyone?* Oh, yes, two teenagers, and a sour-faced woman thumbing through a magazine while her toes were painted blood red.

Blood. Madison shivered at the thought, imagining the blood that had seeped from Brash when the arrows struck.

A mewl of pain escaped her. The thought of her dear husband, lying there on the ground, bleeding...

"Hush, *sha.*"

The words coming from Miss Zuri's lips sounded like an admonishment.

I stand corrected, she idly thought. *It's Madam Zuri. Cajun, just like the words she uses.*

Madison frowned again. This time she knew why.

Was she speaking Cajun French?

Unease slithered down Madison's spine. As the old woman's masterful hands kneaded her flesh, Madison reasoned with herself. She was being silly. It wasn't like Miss Zuri was Madam Zuri, the voodoo queen. The strange words she spoke weren't some sort of *gris gris.* The woman wasn't casting a curse over her, for Heaven's sake! The shop specialized in essential oils and massages, not black magic.

Even so, Madison stiffened. Whatever nibbled on the edge of her brain took a more forceful bite. She remembered bits and pieces of a conversation from her first visit here. She, Shannon, and Megan had been discussing the divine-smelling lotion used.

...Essential oils...

...Herb extracts...

...Secret formulas...

...Handed down from her grandmother, a voodoo priestess...

...Magical spells...

Megan's playful voice as she said, "I hear Cajun

voodoo queens have some superpower that lets them live long lives."

To which Madison teased back, "Unlike their enemies?"

Hoping to clear her thoughts, Madison shook her head.

"This hurts you, *sha*?" Miss Zuri asked.

"No, it's good," Madison answered automatically, but her mind was somewhere else.

The first time she was here, Miss Zuri called her *ma douce*, a French endearment. Today, Madam Zuri called her *cher,* a decidedly Cajun French endearment pronounced *sha*. Did she naturally switch between the two dialects, or did it mean something? And if so, what?

...A special blend of tea...

Unbidden, the thought popped into Madison's mind. More followed.

Delphine Craddock used a special blend of Miss Zuri's teas.

Delphine Craddock suffered from severe mood swings.

Delphine Craddock had hired Madison to keep her from killing someone.

Madison suddenly felt ill. Did Delphine want to kill just *any* someone?

Or *someone wearing a badge?*

23

"I—I don't feel well," Madison told Miss Zuri.

It wasn't a lie. Her stomach roiled, and a cold sweat broke across her skin. Her head pounded in tune with her quickening pulse. As Madison rolled off the table, she felt unusually weak. Had Miss Zuri somehow poisoned her?

Poison!

Madison saw it, now, with sudden clarity. Miss Zuri—Madam Zuri—was behind the attacks on first responders! It made no sense at all, and yet it made perfect sense.

It wasn't just Delphine Craddock.

The first victim remembered smelling something sweet just before being bashed over the head. Miss Zuri specialized in sweet-smelling blends.

A deputy in Cougar Springs was roped and dragged. Moments ago, she had overheard the women in western apparel talking about team roping.

Two medics and one firefighter had been shot, one fatally. Madison remembered now what the 4-H leader coached: shooting events.

A security guard had been injected with unidentified meds. Someone said a nurse frequented the spa.

All were patrons here.

Who had mentioned the nurse, anyway? It had been a conversation over dinner...

Madison all but gasped. *Miss Sybil!*

And yet that, too, somehow made sense, even when the very thought was incomprehensible. Miss Sybil was the sweetest person she knew, but she had been acting so strange lately. Like Delphine, she had sudden bouts of anger and uncharacteristic behavior.

Madison had seen the anger with her own eyes. That day at Wanda Shanks', Miss Sybil had been downright hostile toward Cutter, and even more so toward Otis Perry. They all assumed she had forgotten about the scissors she held when pummeling her fists against his chest, but had she? Or had she been trying to attack the deputy? The same man she was seeing in a clandestine relationship and bringing brownies to?

This time, Madison did gasp. *The brownies!*

Nate ingested poison, and Brash was shot by poison-soaked broad heads.

Could it be? Was dear, sweet Miss Sybil capable of poisoning someone?

Clutching at her stomach, the nausea worsened. The last attack had taken place outside Miss Sybil's house. She had called 9-1-1 and reported a prowler. She claimed to see motorcycles, but there was no evidence of them having been there. She could have simply been mistaken. Or it could have been planned. It could have been a trap for the police.

A trap at her house, Madison reminded herself. Where someone had anchored a trip wire to the side of her house. Where someone had used a bow and at least three arrows to attack the men coming to her rescue. One of those men had been Miss Sybil's supposed boyfriend, and the other had been Madison's beloved husband.

At the thought of Miss Sybil playing a part in Brash's injuries, Madison thought she might lose what little lunch she had eaten.

Fighting off waves of nausea, another piece of the puzzle clicked into place. The man who bought the arrow necklace said his wife was an archer and had sprained her ankle. He also said she was a patron at *Miss Zuri's Essentials.*

There was a woman in the cast waiting by the door. Was that his wife? Had she gotten the injury while shooting a flaming arrow into a dry field? *Was she the one who shot Brash?*

Each of those people had connections to Miss Zuri. Each had expertise in the methods used to attack first responders. In Miss Sybil's case, it was baking, but brownies were one of her specialties.

In a sick, twisted way, it all made sense.

Madison realized *Madam Zuri,* the voodoo priestess of black magic, was watching her closely. The look in her obsidian eyes told Madison everything she needed to know.

Madam Zuri knew that Madison knew.

When Madison moved toward the door, the older woman blocked her path. The music increased in tempo and the Cajun woman chanted more of her strange, unknown words. Madison imagined they were a blend of French, Cajun French, and Creole.

It's not a curse, Madison told herself sternly. *It's a mind game. It's the tribal music, and the lyrical chants, and the way she whispers low in her customers' ears when they're fully relaxed and their guards are down. She plays with their psyche. She brainwashes others to do her bidding.*

Madison's spine straightened in resolve. *I can play mind games, too.*

"Who was it?" Madison asked, her voice surprisingly strong despite feeling so ill.

"Who was what?" the old woman barked.

"Who did you lose?"

"Who said I lost someone? You know nothing, *couyon*."

"Stop it!" Madison snapped. "You're no Cajun voodoo priestess. You're a pathetic old woman out for revenge. Tell me the truth. Who did you lose? And why do you blame all people who wear a badge for your loss?"

Miss Zuri's chest rose and fell with barely controlled rage. If possible, her black eyes darkened even more.

"Again, you are a fool!" she spat. "You know nothing!"

"I know you're too big of a coward to do your own dirty work. You hide behind others, tricking them into doing your bidding. And what for? Some silly vendetta?"

Goaded into an admission, the old woman hissed, "You dare call the death of my only son a silly vendetta?"

Just for a moment, Madison's heart went out to the woman. She had lost a child. Her son. Madison couldn't imagine a pain more horrific.

But her sympathy for Miss Zuri was short-lived. This woman had almost killed Brash, and she had succeeded in killing Jose Robles. Maybe not by her own hand, but she was responsible for the attacks on their valued first responders. It was her hatred and her blind revenge that had caused so much pain and destruction.

"I'm sorry for your loss," Madison said with sincerity, "but why do you take your pain out on innocent people?"

"Innocent? *Innocent?*" she raged. "They killed my boy! He died in my arms after a policeman shot him. I called for an ambulance, but he bled out before they would come to his rescue. They killed him! Don't you understand? They murdered my boy!"

"I can't imagine your pain. Your horror. But surely, you must know the ambulance didn't refuse to come. They always respond."

"They may as well have refused. They were too late. Too late, I tell you!" Her eyes glazed over in unmitigated hate.

"Where, Miss Zuri? Here in The Sisters?"

"Outside of New Orleans. But it doesn't matter. The police are the same anywhere!" she claimed defensively.

"And the firefighters?" Madison asked, softening her voice. "You had a volunteer fireman killed. Shot to death. What did the firefighters do to you? To your son?"

"They claimed he set a fire. An apartment building, where five people died. They called him an arsonist and a murderer!"

Madison took a risk by asking, "And did he? Set the fire, I mean?"

"Of course not!" she said, but Madison saw the truth in her eyes. The uncertainty. The doubt that haunted her to this day.

"How old was your son, Miss Zuri?"

"Nineteen. He was nineteen, and they murdered him! Every one of them!"

"Jose Robles was in his mid-twenties. That was the name of the man you had murdered. You killed an innocent man who had nothing to do with the death of your son. Don't you see? You caused another mother to suffer, the same way you're suffering. Was it worth it? What did you gain by taking another young man's life?"

"Shut up! Shut. Up."

"What did my husband do to you, Miss Zuri? He's

lying in a hospital room right this minute, because *you* chose to punish him for something he did not do." Madison saw the old woman flinch at her words, but now that she had started, she couldn't stop. "*Why?* What possible reason could you have for being so cruel? If you had loved your son at all, you would have honored his memory, not sullied it with your hate and vindictiveness!"

Enraged, Miss Zuri roared out her wrath. Until this moment, Madison had never truly heard a human roar like a bear, but this woman did. The sound was bigger than she was, bellowed with pain and sorrow, and absolute hatred.

It was all directed at Madison.

The old woman charged, catching her off guard. Madison lost her footing and slipped, but she refused to go down without a fight. She grabbed Miss Zuri's flowing caftan and jerked as hard as possible. The other woman came tumbling down, trapping Madison in a swirl of colorful fabric and heady incense. The sweet-smelling oils made Madison's head swim, but she kicked her way free and scrambled from beneath her opponent.

She screamed for help as Miss Zuri lunged again. Suddenly, people were rushing into the massage room. Madison breathed a sigh of relief, but her hopes of being rescued were gone in an instant.

The loyal staff thought Madison was attacking their beloved employer, rather than the other way around. Even the customers took Miss Zuri's side. Someone called 9-1-1, saying there was a crazed woman in the spa, attacking the owner.

"Don't come! It's an ambush!" Madison yelled, hoping her words carried over the din of excited voices.

It took a half dozen people to restrain her, but Madison found herself immobile and at the mercy of these killers. They may have been unintentional killers, but they were killers, nonetheless.

"Don't you see?" Madison cried to those who held her down. "She's been brainwashing you! She's using the music and the herbs and oils to trick you into doing terrible things."

"Do not listen to this woman," Miss Zuri insisted. "She is unwell. A *couyon*. She needs help."

"*You* are the ones who need help." Madison beseeched her captors, pleading for them to understand. "She's been using you to carry out her own sick agenda."

"What are you talking about? You've gone crazy, just like Miss Zuri said," one of the women in the Sticker Pierce boots grumbled, tightening her hold on Madison.

Madison tilted her head toward the woman's friend. "You two are team ropers, right?"

The friend narrowed her eyes. "What if we are? Why would you care?"

"Because she manipulated you. Miss Zuri used you to attack a deputy in Cougar Springs, didn't she?"

"Of—Of course not!"

"She convinced you that all first responders are evil, and she sent you to Cougar Springs. She convinced you to rope a deputy and drag him across the parking lot."

"Don't listen to her, Ruby!" Miss Zuri snapped. In response, the woman's jaw tightened, and her chin nudged forward. "Ignore her. She's crazy," Miss Zuri repeated.

"Am I?" Madison looked at the man holding her by the ankles. Exhausted from fighting her restraints, she used what energy she had left to talk. To make them see the truth. "You help the 4-H group with their shooting skills, don't you?" she asked the man.

He didn't answer, but she forged on.

"Somehow, Miss Zuri conditioned you to hate first responders. She probably told you they were out to harm other people. She convinced you to stop them at all costs. She manipulated you. She *used* you for her own evil!"

The old woman was quick to step in. "Admit nothing. She's trying to trick you. She's accusing you of murdering that firefighter a few weeks ago."

Madison didn't give up. "Ask her about her son." It was the one thing sure to trigger the old woman. The one thing that would reveal her true evil. "Ask her why she hates first responders so much. Why she's determined to destroy them all. That's why she's using you—all of you! —to carry out her own agenda! Just ask her. And ask her what she did to my husband!"

Gladys Peavy spoke in a sharp voice. She played Bunco with Granny Bert, and she had known Brash his entire life. "Brash? She did something to Brash?"

"Yes! She manipulated *that* woman"—because her hands were bound, Madison could only nod to the woman in the cast— "to shoot a poisoned arrow at Brash. Brash, who's been nothing but good and fair and decent to everyone in this town. He's in the hospital, still fighting for his life, because of some woman you barely know!"

She had everyone's attention now. "Most of you have known Brash for years," she hurried on. "This woman has only been in town for a few months, but she's been using you the whole time. She tricked you. She tricked all of you." Madison drew in a much-needed gulp of air. "Go on. Ask her. Ask her about her son."

"Do not speak to me about my boy, you hear me?" Miss Zuri snarled the words as she gave Madison a deadly glare. "Don't forget who I am."

"I know who you are. You're a bitter old woman who

suffered a tragic loss, but you're turning your hatred on innocent people. What's worse, you're using innocent people to do your bidding."

In a cold voice, the woman threatened, "I will destroy you. Right this minute." She closed her eyes and began to chant, using her lyrical voice to spin an evil web around the very people holding Madison down.

It wasn't black magic. It was manipulation of the mind. Some sort of hypnosis. The tribal-like music was part of it. The surround-sound acoustics were like a living, breathing thing, and they reinforced the mystical quality in Miss Zuri's voice.

No longer susceptible to her conniving ways, Madison detected the hidden messages scattered in among the odd words and the pagan-sounding phrases. Her whispered words were barely audible. "She is the enemy."

There was another chant, another whispered command. "You know what to do."

After a hummed stanza—this one soft and oddly peaceful—and another chanted chorus, she breathed a deadly directive just under her breath. "Kill her."

The thrumming music suddenly stopped. Miss Zuri's eyes popped opened, and she faltered, stopping mid-chant.

It was enough to ruin the moment. The spell she had woven among her worshipers was unraveling.

There was no other way to describe them, Madison realized. These people worshipped Miss Zuri and would do whatever she asked of them. Including murder.

"Is it true?" The words rang out from the other room. As the familiar voice drew closer, Madison saw Miss Sybil walk into the room. *This* was the Sybil that Madison knew and loved.

But even this Sybil revealed another side of her that Madison had never seen. Miss Sybil's slight body had never stood so erect. Her soft voice had never sounded so strong.

Meek, gentle Sybil was now strong, betrayed Sybil.

"Did you do those vile things?" she demanded. "Did *we* do those vile things?"

Even though Miss Zuri stood a good seven inches over the other woman, she cowered in fear when she saw the look in Sybil's eyes.

"How dare you. How *dare* you!" Miss Sybil raged. "We trusted you!" She advanced toward Miss Zuri. "It was in the tea, wasn't it? Something to make us believe your lies. Something that let you get inside our heads." The closer she came, the more Miss Zuri cowered. "And that 'special vanilla' you gave me for the brownies. It was poison, wasn't it? You said it was the last few drops of your private stash. You told me it was an exotic extract you couldn't get from just anywhere. You told me to make brownies with it and take it to the police station, to show your appreciation for all they do. You had me *poison* them!" Enraged, Sybil reached for a bottle of essential oil. "These oils! They have some sort of loco weed in them, don't they? Something that made us all crazy enough to believe you!" She opened the top and flung the contents into her traitor's face.

"Don't! That's poison!" Miss Zuri cried, putting her hands up in an effort to cover her face.

After her admission, everything happened in a swirl of activity. The people who held Madison immobile suddenly released her, grabbing for the other woman.

The woman who claimed to live a life of purpose.

The woman who supposedly shared 'the secret of natural healing.'

The impostor.

Madison made a quick call to Vina, explaining the

situation in as few words as possible. Vina would take it from there.

When she hung up, Miss Sybil was there beside her, broken and crying.

"Oh, Madison! How could I do it? How could I do that to the people I love? I-I almost got Brash killed. How can you ever forgive me? How can I ever forgive myself?"

Madison pulled the old woman to her in a tight hug. "I forgive you because I love you, and because I know it wasn't your fault. She used you. She manipulated you. I know you would never do those things on your own. You don't have an evil bone in your body, Miss Sybil."

"I'm so sorry!" she sobbed, clinging to Madison as her strength failed her. "I'm so, so sorry! So sorry."

"Shh, Miss Sybil. It's over now. Everything will be fine."

"But... Brash! You said he was fighting for his life!"

A smile broke through Madison's own tears. "Do you really think I'd be here if his life were hanging in the balance? He's still very weak and has a long road of recovery, but the doctors are confident he'll be fine in time."

"Truly? You aren't just saying that to make me feel better?"

"I may have embellished that part, but I'm telling you the truth, Miss Sybil. Especially about not leaving him if he wasn't out of the woods. Today is the first time I've felt confident enough to leave the hospital. I promise you that I'm telling the truth."

Miss Sybil surprised her yet again. With tears still wet on her face, the old woman threw back her head and laughed. It was the first real laugh Madison had heard from her in weeks. "You little stinker, you, 'embellishing' like that! Bertha will be so proud when I tell her!"

24

By the time Madison returned to the hospital that evening, it was late.

Technically, visiting hours were over. Madison came in through the emergency room entrance and hurried upstairs.

Most of the family was still there. They needed to see that she had come through the ordeal unscathed, and to hear her version of what really happened. The rumors had already started and were drifting their way.

Madison perched on the side of her husband's bed and unraveled the twisted story.

"And no," she concluded, "the motorcycle guys weren't part of this. And they definitely didn't ride into the spa and wreak havoc like some of the rumors say."

"It would be easier to believe they did this, than Miss Zuri," Megan wailed. "And to think, I actually loved that place."

"I never even got a chance to go," Bethani lamented.

"Well," Granny Bert huffed, "it doesn't surprise me one bit. I told you there was some sort of black magic going on in there. I told you she was mixing potions, along with all her herbs and lotions."

"She wasn't using potions," Madison said with a

frown. "Not per se. She was using mind games, though. She got her subjects all relaxed and cozy, with their defenses down and their inhibitions low, and she whispered ideas into their heads. I heard it. It was... eerie. Intriguing, to be truthful, but tragic because it worked."

"Like what?" Lydia wanted to know. "How did she do something like that?"

"And how could people be gullible?" Her husband's tone was gruff with scorn. To the rugged rancher, none of it made sense.

"I'm sure you've never had a massage, Papa D—" Madison started. When she saw the smile on her mother-in-law's face and the faint stain on Andrew's cheeks, she tried hiding her surprise. "Or maybe you have," she quickly corrected. "It's such a relaxing experience. You feel like you don't have a care in the world. And I have to admit that Miss Zuri has a very lyrical-sounding voice. Her accent is so exotic, or it is when she's trying to lure you into her spell."

"See!" Granny Bert interrupted. "She uses spells! Like I said, voodoo and black magic."

Ignoring the comment, Madison continued. It was difficult to describe the hold Miss Zuri had on her followers, and the methods she used so effectively. Like it or not, the woman was definitely talented when it came to manipulating them in such a seemingly innocuous way.

"She does this mesmerizing chant, while some sort of tribal-like music plays. It doesn't sound evil. It sounds almost spiritual. Isn't that what you thought, Megan?" She looked to her stepdaughter for confirmation.

Megan nodded, her auburn-red hair dancing around her shoulders. "It's almost like a pagan ceremony of sorts. There's a raw energy to it. It sort of wraps around you and pulls you in."

"Exactly. And then she starts to chant, her voice a blend of French and Cajun accents that sounds almost magical." Madison closed her eyes, trying to recreate the feeling for her audience. Her voice softened as she spoke. She gently swayed back and forth. "It's very exotic and peaceful, like you're somewhere far off on a tropical island. Even the language she uses is exotic. A mix of French and Cajun and Creole. The more she chants, the more the words blend together into a spellbinding hum."

Then Madison opened her eyes, and her voice hardened. "But today, I wasn't so relaxed. I was on alert, and my defenses weren't down. And I heard some of what she was actually saying. Somewhere among the chants and the humming, she slipped in English words. Dangerous words. Like 'she's the enemy,' and 'you know what to do.' But the most chilling of all was when she said, 'kill her.'"

Brash had been drifting in and out of sleep. The company was nice, but it had been a long day. He was still weak and in quite a bit of pain. He told the nurses it wasn't bad, but the truth was that he didn't want to be completely knocked out. He hated being defenseless, especially when he heard what Maddy had been through that day.

She thought he slept through her story, but his eyes opened into a slit, and he spoke in a voice that was rusty and rough. "You could have been killed."

"But I wasn't, Brash," she said softly. Her fingers entwined with his. "I'm fine. Miss Sybil came to my rescue."

Blake shook his head in amazement. "I still can't imagine meek little Miss Sybil doing something like that. She's always been the sensible one of the lot. I always thought she kept Granny Bert and the others in line, but now I'm not so sure."

"She's been my best friend for eighty years," Granny Bert boasted. "Don't you think she's learned a thing or two from me in all those years? There's a time to go along, and there's a time to stand up. Today, she stood up in a big way."

"Absolutely," Lydia agreed. "And she saved our dear Madison, and only the good Lord knows how many others."

Granny Bert sent Madison a sly look. Her eyes twinkled with pride. "I hear there may have been a little grandstanding on Maddy's part. She led them to believe Brash was practically on his deathbed. I think the shock brought Sybil out of her trance and made her stand up like she did."

"Like you said, Granny," Madison admitted with a laugh, "you tend to rub off on people after a while. You've been known to spin a yarn or two to make your point."

She simply shrugged. "Like I said, sometimes you have to stand up, even if it means telling a little white lie."

"I hate to admit it, but you're right." Madison darted her eyes around the room and issued a disclaimer. "Kids, don't try this at home."

"Wait," Blake said, as a troubling thought occurred to him. "What about her other clients? What if she's already brainwashed them, and they still do something else? Can anyone stop them?"

"That's a valid concern," his mom acknowledged. "The sheriff confiscated her list of clients and appointment book. One of the agencies—I think the US Marshal Service, but I might be wrong—are already contacting the families of each client to tell them of the situation. The agency will set up observation sessions for everyone involved and help create a treatment plan for those showing signs of having been brainwashed. It's not a fool-proof plan, but it's better than having Miss Zuri pumping that jargon into their minds."

"Will the people who carried out her plans be punished?" Megan asked. Her eyes went to her father, who had unwillingly drifted off to sleep again. "Like the woman who did this to him? She may have been acting under the influence, but she was still the one to pull the bow string and put him in this place."

"I honestly don't know," Madison admitted. "I suppose that's up to the courts to decide. Miss Zuri, I'm sure, will spend the rest of her life in prison."

Andrew put his two cents in with a skeptical snort. "You can bet they'll hire some highfaluting lawyer, trying to avoid a prison sentence."

Bethani looked concerned. "You mean Miss Sybil could go to prison?"

"That's not for us to say," Granny Bert answered. "I imagine her stopping that woman will go a long way in exonerating her." She looked over at Madison. "I suppose Delphine Craddock deserves some credit, too. She helped you put two and two together and make the connection."

"Who's Delphine Craddock?" Bethani asked.

"The woman who hired me to keep her from hurting someone. She didn't know who, just that she would feel an incredible rage come over her for no reason at all. I don't think she ever acted on her rage."

"The one we saw at *Montelongo's*?" Megan recognized the name. "She definitely acted weird that night."

"I thought it was because Nate came up, and she thought you were shunning her grandson. Now I realize it was Nate's uniform that set her off."

"In a totally weird way, I guess that makes sense."

Blake wasn't listening to their exchange. He was

still worried about Miss Sybil.

"Do you think we could act as character witnesses for her?" Blake asked.

Megan was confused by the question. "For Delphine Craddock?"

"Who?" He frowned. "I'm talking about Miss Sybil."

"I'll do it!" his twin agreed.

Megan was hesitant to get on board. Miss Sybil admitted to baking the brownies that poisoned her boyfriend. It was still unclear as to who poisoned the arrows.

Madison understood her hesitation. She felt torn between her love for her husband and her love for a woman she considered part of the family. Brash won, of course, but she still felt compassion for Miss Sybil.

"It certainly couldn't hurt," she agreed. "We all know that she would never have done this on her own. Especially not to your father. She loves Brash."

"You're right," Megan spoke up softly. "I'll vouch for her, too, if you think it will help."

Madison was proud of her stepdaughter, and it showed in her tender smile. "It may not come to a court of law, but I'm sure there will be some sort of inquisition. Our support will probably go a long way in determining her fate."

Everyone was silent for a moment, pondering the possibility that Miss Sybil could face some sort of punishment. It was a complicated situation, hoping one woman was exonerated, while hoping another faced severe consequences for her actions. It wasn't just the shop owner. The woman who shot Brash should pay, as well.

"There's something else I'm curious about," Lydia said with a frown. "Why wasn't Wanda Shanks affected by all this?"

"From what I understand," Madison said, "Miss

Zuri hand-picked her subjects after learning about their particular skills. When she found out the one woman was into archery, she devised a plan to use a bow and arrows in her attacks. The same with the man who coached shooting sports with the 4H Club, and with Miss Sybil, who was known for her cooking skills and who often sent treats to the police station. I suspect that"—her lips quirked with a barely suppressed smile— "she didn't find any particular skills she could exploit with Miss Wanda. I think she's too much of a loose cannon to rely on for something like this."

"It's actually fascinating that Miss Zuri could pull off something like this off," Blake said, "in a disgusting, repulsive sort of way."

"That's exactly what I thought. After witnessing it firsthand, I do get where she could instill prejudice against people wearing a badge, but it's hard to make the leap on how she convinced them to take specific action. How do you convince an otherwise law-abiding, easygoing person to commit such heinous crimes? It's hard to comprehend."

"All I can say is, the woman is filled with hate and revenge," Andrew practically spat. "I know how hard it must be to lose a child—this ordeal with Brash has been bad enough on us—but that's no reason to make other parents and families suffer, too. That woman deserves to rot in prison. *I'll* sign up to be the first one to speak on her behalf. And it won't be positive!"

"I'll be right behind you, Pops," Blake agreed.

With the hour growing late, and Brash now sleeping peacefully, his parents and Granny Bert left. The kids were slower to say their evening goodbyes.

They stood around Brash's bedside, thinking about all the ways things could have gone differently.

If Cutter's crew and the ambulance hadn't gotten there so quickly. If the arrow had been one inch lower.

If infection had set in.

If the poison had been more deadly.

If the surgeons had been less skilled.

If he hadn't been strong enough to fight the odds and survive.

The 'ifs' haunted them, but the victories made up for it. He had lived, and there was every reason to believe that, in time, he would make a full recovery.

Blake and Megan stood on one side of the bed, with Bethani on the other.

There had been a time when Bethani resented the new man in their life, but she had come to love and depend on her stepfather. Even though she had been 'daddy's little girl' when Gray was alive, that daddy had betrayed them all by breaking his marriage vows and tearing their family apart. Somehow, she knew that Daddy D wasn't that kind of man. He would never do that to her mother, or to their family. Because that's exactly what they were. A family. *His* family. And he was theirs.

Madison came up beside her daughter, sliding an arm around her waist as they all gazed down at the man they loved.

"Thank all of you for being here through all of this," Madison said softly. "It's meant so much to him, knowing he had your support. Knowing that, if the worst had happened, we would stick together and have each other to fall back on. I think he's been more worried about what would happen to *us* than he has been about what would happen to him."

Sniffing away tears, Megan nodded. "It's always been that way, you know. Even before he became a police officer. He's always looked out for the people he loved. And once he pinned that badge on, he did it for people he didn't even know. He vowed to protect and serve, and that's exactly what he's done. He hasn't worried so much about himself. He just wants to do the right thing and protect the people around him."

"Well said, sweetheart. And until all this happened, I never realized just how heavy that badge was," Madison admitted. "I knew he carried a lot of responsibility, a lot of weight on his shoulders. I knew that every time he stopped a motorist or walked into a domestic argument or dealt with criminals that he was facing a risk, but this whole situation has really hit home."

"It took a lot of guts," Blake agreed, "to go out there when first responders were coming under attack. They were all taking a big risk. I don't know if I could have done it. I don't know if I'm brave enough to pin on a badge, or a firefighter or paramedic uniform, and risk my life like that."

They assumed Brash was soundly asleep. His eyes were still closed. When he spoke, his voice was quiet and low. "It doesn't weigh all that much. You could bear it."

"We didn't mean to wake you, sweetheart," Madison said. She stroked his stubbled jaw with loving care. He hadn't been able to shave, and she rather liked the new beard. In her eyes, it made him even more rakishly handsome, pale skin and all.

"My family's never a bother."

"We love you so much, Daddy D," Bethani said. "We can't wait to have you back home."

"Can't wait to be there."

"I love you, Daddy," Megan said with a squeeze to his hand. "I'm so proud of you, and what you do. How you stand up for your family and your community and how you keep us all safe."

"Ditto," Blake agreed. His blue eyes glistened with unshed tears.

"This is starting to sound more like a eulogy than a

pep talk," Brash grumbled. But a new gruffness in his voice told them he was touched by their words.

"In that case, allow me to lighten the mood," Blake volunteered, ever the comic out of the group. "There's a new baseball glove I want, and it only costs a couple hundred bucks. Think you could buy it for your favorite son?"

"Ooh, and I saw the cutest little purse the other day!" Megan pitched in. "It carried a big price tag, but I figured it might be like that shiny little badge of yours. Heavy, but so worth it!"

Bethani couldn't be left out. "And I need a coat for winter. You never know when we might get lucky and drop below tropical heat levels. I saw this amazing one at Neiman Marcus. It's out of this poor college girl's price range, but she happens to have this wonderful, generous father who just loves buying her gifts. So, what do you say?"

"I say y'all are making me laugh, and it hurts."

"Mom, you didn't say what's on your wish list," Blake said. "Christmas will be here soon, so we're just giving him a few shopping ideas. You may as well join in."

"No need," she said. She gazed down at her husband with a smile. "I have everything I could ever hope for, right here in this room."

Note from the Author

Thank you for visiting our cozy little The Sisters, Texas community! I hope you come back often for a visit, especially on April 19 when another exciting debut rolls into town!

Also, thank you for reading this book. I realize that without you, this would simply be a fun (although expensive) hobby. With you, I'm living my dream of being an author.

I know, I hate this part too, because it's almost like I'm asking for a gift. But if you enjoyed my tale, please take a moment to write a brief review on Amazon, Bookbub, Goodreads, and/or the platform of your choice. Reviews play such a pivotal role in an author's career. Reviews are how readers find us, how Amazon rates us, and, best of all, they're how we authors know if we're on the right track.

After leaving your review, please feel free to drop me a personal note. (Your notes are the best part of being an author!) Here's how you can reach me:
beckiwillis.ccp@gmail.com
www.beckiwillis.com
http://www.facebook.com/beckiwillis.ccp/

ABOUT THE AUTHOR

Becki Willis, best known for her popular The Sisters, Texas Mystery Series, Forgotten Boxes, and Keep Your Doors Locked is a best-selling who has won numerous awards. These include two Silver Falchions Awards, a RONE, first place honors for Best Mystery Series, Best Suspense Fiction and Best Audio Book, and many more. She has introduced her imaginary friends to readers around the world.

An avid history buff, Becki likes to poke around in old places and learn about the past. Other addictions include reading, writing, unraveling a good mystery, and coffee. She loves to travel but believes coming home to her family and her Texas ranch is the best part of any trip. Becki attended Texas A&M University and majored in Journalism.

Connect with her at http://www.beckiwillis.com/ or http://www.facebook.com/beckiwillis.ccp.

Better yet, email her at beckiwillis.ccp@gmail.com. She loves to hear from readers and encourages feedback!

www.ingramcontent.com/pod-product-compliance
Lightning Source LLC
Chambersburg PA
CBHW061241210726

48293CB00003B/852